Copyright © 2024

All rights reserved.

This is a work of fiction. Any resemblance to actual people, places, institutions, families etc is entirely coincidental.

This book is copyright material. No part of this book may be copied, reproduced, transferred, distributed, leased, licensed or publicly performed or used in any way except as specifically permitted in writing by the author.

NIGHT TERRORS

Short Stories to Read After Dark

By Maraya Ashworth

Dedication -

To those who know that nothing is more scary than real life.

Content + Trigger Warnings

Although this book contains fictional horror stories, it does address real-life harmful and distressing themes, as well as some supernatural craziness. Proceed with caution and read responsibly.

This book is intended to be gut-wrenching and spine-tingling!

Costume Party
- Kidnapping
- Drugging
- Alcohol Abuse
- Violence
- Purging (I apologise if I ruin Gummy Bears)
- Burning
- Assault and battery
- Death

The Devil on the Dance Floor
- Rape (on page)
- Murder
- Stalking
- Kidnapping
- Knife Play

- Drugging
- Sex
- Sexual Assault
- Gore

Coming for Me
- Stalking
- Death
- Drugs

Risky Research
- Blood
- Threat to life
- Mild Gore

New Friends, New Sins
- Bullying
- Death
- Gore

Costume Party

The cool, damp air is unbearable in the rotten basement of Jason's farmhouse. Maria falls back onto the rickety bed, the mattress barely covering the metal springs that dig into her bones. She contemplates what time of day it could be and comes up short. The only indicator of time passing is the relentless boredom and her grumbling stomach that threatens to digest itself and all her other organs. Hope is a distant memory. Maria is ready for it all to end. She has lost count of how many days she has been trapped in this awful, cramped space with only a bed and bucket on the slimy concrete floor. Like every day, she blankly stares at the ceiling, considering how large the mould spores have grown since she was first thrown in here. The smell is barely noticeable now, though at first, it was stifling and made her nauseous.

Jason let her out once before to test her obedience. It was a late summer evening, she hadn't showered in days, maybe even weeks. Her slick hair clung to her forehead and shoulders as she wrapped her arms around herself in an attempt for comfort. He dropped her off in the middle of a large field where people were camping and forced her to approach them and ask for a drink. He fiercely warned her that if she tried to escape or told them that she was a missing person, he would catch her and kill her.

    Starved from days of eating a cereal bar for lunch and dinner, she felt too frail to run and even more scared to speak up for fear of the consequences. So, she did what he asked. When she neared the campers, she realised they were young men, drunk and possibly on drugs. They circled her, checking her out and whistling to one another as they humiliated her. They shoved a beer bottle into her hand and asked her to sit with them. Frightened, she looked around and saw two flashes of headlights in the distance indicating it was time to return to Jason. She thanked the men and raced back to the car claiming her boyfriend was waiting, hating herself for feeling safer leaving the group of disorderly men. Jason sat with a smug look on his face as he watched her climb back into the car, shaking and defeated.

    Since then, she has been trapped in the basement waiting for the next awful thing; wishing for a swift end to her miserable existence.

It wasn't always like this. Months ago, she was a happy-go-lucky college student, meeting new people, trying new hobbies, and working towards her dream of becoming a drama teacher. Since Maria was seven, it was her dream to teach and inspire young minds and everything was going according to plan. There was just one thing missing. She craved companionship. No one had ever given her the attention she so desperately needed. Her mother always told her that she was like a fish trapped in an aquarium and one day another fish would be captured and placed in her tank and they would fall in love. The irony. If she'd known it was a premonition, she would have avoided men altogether.

Despite her mother's offensive remark at her failure to garner any male attention, she did *eventually* fall for someone.

One night, towards the end of the last semester of her second year at university, her friends dragged her on a night out. It was the only time she ever drank more than two drinks. Hangovers were something Maria was always afraid of. She hated not feeling one hundred per cent and despised wasting the day even more. However, that night she needed the extra courage to step out of her comfort zone and put her heart on the line.

The night went by remarkably unsuccessfully until they reached the last bar. Upon entering, her eyes immediately locked with the most handsome man she had ever seen. He was tall and slim with impeccable taste in clothes and a five o'clock shadow that gave him the perfect rugged look, while still being presentable. Gulping down her insecurities, she puffed out her chest and approached him. His charming smile grew as she neared and her shoulders relaxed. The rest of the night was amazing; full of dancing, white wine spritzers, kissing, and more dancing until she was too tired to walk on her swollen feet. Maria and Jason exchanged numbers and went home giddy about their evening.

The next few weeks consisted of the most wonderful dates; walks in the park, coffee in bookshops, dinner in the most beautiful sought-after restaurants, and cosy nights in at Jason's beautiful, rustic farmhouse. Maria had officially been swept off her feet. Jason was her dream man and he said all the right things, complimented parts of her she never even noticed, and made her feel beautiful and interesting. He had ambition and talked about his passions with a bright smile and she watched each time as the corners of his eyes creased a little when he really got into the conversation. She fell in love with him and she had to tell him.

Maria organised the perfect evening; she texted Jason and told him she wanted him to meet her parents. She hadn't told them about him yet and wanted to do it soon. Jason convinced her to hold off telling them because it would be more exciting to surprise them with a visit. Maria felt elated. Until the next day while passing the local cafe outside of her university building, Maria saw him. He was leaning on his car with another woman pressed between his legs. The woman was gorgeous; with long white-blonde hair, a womanly figure, and dressed in a beautiful tartan blazer and skirt co-ord. Maria froze mouth agape, and watched as he reached his hand behind her head, bringing her in for a delicate kiss. Unable to watch any more, she raced home and cried and cried until there were no tears left. She took out her phone and texted Jason to wish him well but that she would not be seeing him again. On the bright side, she hadn't yet told her parents about him, only to have to embarrassingly confess it was over already.

For the next few days, her phone blew up with messages and calls; Jason begging her to forgive him and let him explain. He wrote essay-length messages about how much he cared for her and confessed that he was saying goodbye to an old 'situationship'. He stated repeatedly that he only wanted to be with her. Eventually, Maria relented and agreed to meet up with him to test how she felt upon seeing him. She chose somewhere public because she wanted to avoid the temptation to be intimate with him, to let him close enough to disarm her.

Jason let her pick the venue and she chose a casual bar in the middle of their homes so they both travelled an equal distance. They talked for an hour and she told him how much it hurt to see him kiss another woman. He confessed his love and apologised, begging for one more chance. By the end of it, Maria took a deep breath and contemplated his words. Ultimately, she decided she needed more time to process her feelings because the image of him kissing that woman still stung. Jason calmly accepted her decision and offered to drive her home. Maria agreed and they headed towards his car. In a gentlemanly manner, Jason opened the car door for her and closed it once she was comfortably seated inside. Then he climbed into the driver's seat and looked over at Maria with dark eyes. Something had changed. His defeated expression had turned cold and Maria recoiled in confusion. Changing her mind about accepting the lift, she told him she'd prefer to walk home. However, when she tried to open the door it was locked. The child locks had been activated. As she faced him, a tiny pinprick stung her arm. A few drowsy minutes passed and that was all Maria could remember. When she woke she was locked in this basement, with no windows or fresh air; just a bed and a bucket to relieve herself. Hours went by before Jason delivered a bottle of water and a sandwich. She pleaded with him to let her go, wailing and flailing her arms but he shoved her onto the bed, pinned her down and threatened to kill her if she ever rejected him like that again. Then he left her sobbing into her arms in the fetal position and didn't return for nearly two days.

    Since that day, Maria has grown used to the long hours of silence and isolation. She has worn out all her mental games and activities, like counting the mould spots on the ceiling, counting the bricks on the wall, and trying to break the metal handle off of the bucket to form some kind of key or weapon. Nothing has worked to help her escape or cure her boredom.

The clinking of keys has Maria bolting upright. Jason's visits are few and far between, likely due to his demanding work schedule. He makes short trips to leave her with a loaf of bread, packets of ham, and bottles of water, which she must ration without knowing when he will be back. Occasionally he comes in while she is sleeping and is too weak to sit up, and he torments her by tracing his fingers up her back and stroking her hair, then leaves again. It makes her skin crawl.

This time, he throws down a large shopping bag and nods towards it with a cheerful grin on his cleanly-shaven face. She stills, wishing for the bag to contain clean clothes. She would kill for a shower. Apprehension thick in the air, Maria shuffles off the bed and peers into the bag, pulling out a sexy pumpkin costume that looks two sizes too small.

"Put it on," Jason demands. Judging by the costume, it is apparent that Halloween has rolled around, which means she's been here for over two months.

So far, Jason hadn't taken things too far. Kidnapping, starving and humiliation aside, Maria felt grateful he hadn't forced her to do anything more with him. He didn't seem interested in touching her like that and as painful as it was to be trapped by this psychopath, she felt lucky not to have been subjected to him in that way. Although, the fear of it was planted in the back of her mind. In the beginning, for a whole week, Jason arrived with a new costume each day and threatened her to perform a one-woman musical about cats, dressed as a dog; he brought her a magician's coat and a children's magic set and made her put on a show; then he brought socks and craft supplies and had her perform with sock-puppets. All of it was utterly degrading and psychotic, but it saved her from the threat of physical pain and each night she was rewarded with food. It was a shame she was too nauseous to eat it.

She holds the costume up against her body, cringing. Knowing it means Jason is ready for another show, she tries to imagine what she'll be expected to do. When Maria is finished getting dressed as a pumpkin, the length of it barely covering her underwear, Jason hands her two pots of face paint in orange and black and leaves the room.

As Maria trudges up the stairs to the ground floor, Jason sniggers at her haphazard attempt to put on the paint without a mirror. Maria folds in on herself, praying for the ground to swallow her up. Undeterred by her discomfort, Jason shoves her towards his car and explains that he wants her to go trick or treating in the nearby village. Reminding her that one wrong move and she is dead.

They pull up outside of the first house, decorated extravagantly with police tape, cobwebs, gravestones, and skeletons. Halloween has always been Maria's favourite holiday. It is the only one void of any pressure to be with family, to buy gifts, or to plan months in advance. This holiday doesn't belong to anyone, so each year she can do something different. However now, even if she made it out of this alive, she would never celebrate Halloween again.

Maria reluctantly inches her way to the door, passing some children giggling and marvelling over their score of treats. When she arrives at the door, eyes welling and hands shaking, she knocks softly. A middle-aged woman greets her with a welcoming smile and a bowl full of sweets. Maria clears her throat and stares at the woman, pleading with her eyes to understand that she needs help, but the woman simply laughs at her costume, throws some sherbet sweets into her cauldron bucket and closes the door. Maria's throat tightens, her lungs unable to suck in oxygen. Her failure is like a knife to her gut. Jason whistles out of his car window, then indicates for her to move on to the next door. They repeat this for several houses until he clicks his fingers at her and points to the car. With every failed house visit, her panic swells, and her chest heaves rapidly. Still, she does not say a word, desperate for someone to recognise her silent pleas. But, no one does. Every happy homeowner opens their door, loads her up with treats and sends her on her merry way. Blow after blow of rejection is more devastating and heartbreaking than the last. Time runs out and no one rescues her or recognises her as a missing girl eager to get home. The grief is too much. On the journey back to the farmhouse, tears smear her painted face, dripping orange and black onto her lap, while Jason's firm grip never leaves her thigh.

    Back in the basement, Jason pours the sweets and chocolate onto the floor. Sitting on the step in the doorway he huffs a laugh amused at himself.

    "Eat it." He commands. "All of it." Maria snaps her head to him from her spot on the bed. "I can't eat all that," she chokes out, sniffling.

    "Do it, now." Jason snatches a chocolate bar from the pile, tears off the wrapper and forces it into her hand. "Eat." Maria takes a small bite of the chocolate bar, its sickly sweet taste coating her mouth. Each chew is like cement and it takes several attempts to swallow the thick paste. Jason impatiently growls at her, then leans over and rams it into her mouth. Choking and spluttering Maria gags, her eyes streaming and face blushing with heat. When the whole bar has been swallowed, Jason hands her the next piece.

An eternity drags on, and with over half the sweets stuffed into her belly, Jason rests a pack of gummy bears on the edge of the bed. With a lead stomach and blazing headache, Maria tentatively opens the packaging. In a slow swaying movement, she lifts one gummy bear to her lips, acid rising in her throat and cramps punching her insides. Jason motions for her to carry on, so she puts the sugary lump into her mouth and reluctantly chews. A bubbling sensation stirs in her gut, sweat beads on her brows, and saliva coats her mouth. Maria knows what's coming and she welcomes it. A second later, she hurtles off the bed, grabs the cauldron with both hands and unleashes the contents of her stomach with an ungodly force. Chunky, gelatinous vomit flies out of her mouth, blocking her airways, and bile seeps out of her nostrils as each wave crashes over the edge.

When the contents of her stomach begins

brimming the edge of the small bucket, Maria finally takes some deep breaths and sits back down on the bed. The putrid smell of jelly sweets and hazelnut praline permeates the air. Jason rises from the step clapping slowly at her efforts before leaving her to stew in the mess. Maria wipes the sour liquid from her chin with her sleeve and leans against the cool wall. Her stomach cramps and groans with unease and she closes her eyes to steady her headache.

    Hours later Maria is lying on her bed, each spring like a bag of nails beneath her, wondering if her parents know she is missing yet or if her friends have contacted the police. The village she had just been in, silently begging people to read the desperate pleas in her eyes, didn't show any indication anyone was looking for her. No missing posters or police patrols, no one she knew wandering the streets. The village is only a few miles from the town she lives in and Jason's house is in the middle of the two. Regret fills her core at her stupidity. Why didn't she tell anyone about him? Even if someone notices her absence, they don't know about Jason and won't know to look here. And what about her job? She hasn't shown up to work for months, they will think she has quit without notice and she has no contract so it's unlikely they will even bat an eye at an unreliable student not showing up. If tonight is Halloween, that means she has missed four weeks of university and is likely failing her classes. She hasn't met any of her new lecturers yet; they must think she is one of them lazy students who only shows up when she feels like it or for exams. Though if she ever got out of here, would she even go back? Could she stay in this town, the very place where her safety and life have been stolen from her?

The exhaustion of the evening sits heavy on her chest and tears spring to Maria's eyes as she frets about her future, the very future she may not have. With each quiet sob, her eyes grow heavy until darkness descends.

A few days later, the basement door swings open and Jason staggers into the enclosure. The stale stench of bourbon envelopes Maria, attacking her senses. He launches another costume at her, slurring his words when he orders her to put it on. Then he impatiently stomps up the stairs to wait for her, kicking the cauldron of vomit over in his drunken haste. Maria gags; the room already reeks and now the putrid, lumpy liquid is spreading across the floor. In a race to get some fresh air, she throws the costume on without registering what it is.

At the top of the stairs, Jason grins like a Cheshire Cat. Maria shudders, she hasn't seen that look before. When she looks down at her frumpy outfit, her face contorts with confusion.

"What am I?" She pulls at her costume examining it. Contemplating it for a moment; it looks like Victorian men's attire.

"Come on." Jason grabs her wrist and pulls her outside. On wobbly legs, she stumbles after him, his tight grip burning her skin. Nearing the long narrow garden, realisation dawns on her like the moment in a horror film when the main character realises they are doomed. The bonfire at the back of the garden burns brighter than the sun. The smoke is billowing out, curling and weaving like dementors. Heat warms her cheeks from all that distance away and her knees almost buckle beneath her. She isn't dressed as a Victorian, she knows her history, this is Elizabethan and she is dressed as Guy Fawkes. No man in his right mind would throw her onto that fire, but Jason is not in his right mind. His hate for Maria is burning away the last shreds of his sanity, her rejection scarring his soul.

Jason shoves her forward, smirking and

gesturing for her to approach the fire.

"Stand in front of it," he demands. A wave of relief washes over her at not burning at the stake. Only the feeling is fleeting as she has no idea what is in store for her.

In front of the blazing fire, the heat beats down on her back, sparks spitting on her costume and the back of her head. Smoke and soot invade her senses and her lungs protest urging her to cough. Distracted, she doesn't see what Jason is doing beyond the black fog until it is too late. A foreign object whooshes past her and into the mountain of flames before exploding with an almighty bang and flash of lights. Maria yelps and dives out of the way as splinters of wood shoot out in all directions.

"Stand up!" Jason booms.

She carefully rises from her protective position on the floor just as another rocket launches into her side, erupting into a crackle of bright lights and searing pain. The shrapnel of fireworks burns her cheek and the smell of singed fabric permeates the air. Maria cries out for Jason to stop but he roars with laughter lighting another firework. The onslaught of blasts comes more rapidly as he sets them off one after the other, howling and jumping with each successful hit. Maria dances and dodges like a jester, and in an attempt to protect her face, she doesn't dare to look up. The cloud of smoke billows all around, suffocating her, and each firework that misses explodes in the inferno behind her, spitting shards of wood and fireballs at her. Utterly surrounded and with no way out, Maria curls up on the floor, huddled as tightly as possible trying to become invisible.

Eventually, the fireworks stop ploughing into her, yet she remains where she is, not so much as flinching. After a few excruciating minutes, footsteps stomp closer. Maria holds her breath, anticipating another blow. Halting in front of her, Jason dumps a barrel of ice-cold water on her. Maria squeals as it bites into her tender flesh. The shock is hellish for a moment before the welcome cold soothes her blistering flesh.

Back in the hell hole she has been trapped in for far too long, Jason leaves her with salve and medicine to help heal her raw, tender skin.

Weeks go by and the torment stops. Maria wonders if Jason is growing bored of her or if he feels guilty for torturing her so badly on bonfire night. She ponders if this is the first time he has done this and if not, what happened to the poor girl in the end. The thought is too frightening, so she shoves it out of her mind. She can't think of something so terrible happening to someone else and she certainly doesn't want to contemplate not making it out of this alive.

The scraps of food he has dropped off every other day haven't been nearly enough. The bones on her shoulders are protruding from her skin; sharp angles have taken over her body. Her hips jut out beneath her trousers and her cheekbones are razor-sharp. Day after day Maria agonises about her family, hoping that someone is missing her, that the police have traced her phone or read her messages. That at the very least Jason is on their radar.

She heard shuffling feet a few nights ago and she prayed to all the Gods that it was the police searching his house, but a few minutes later they retreated and nothing came of it.

Tears were no longer able to form in her malnourished body, so she lay hugging her legs with a heavy chest and foggy mind, losing herself in a deep depression. Scars were beginning to form on her cheek, arms and the side of her torso where the blasts of heat charred her skin. Yet, she felt lucky they hadn't become infected. She hated that she felt grateful for the medicine and enraged that she let this go on for so long without trying to get out. But she wracked her brain every day trying to pull a plan together and nothing materialised. There was no realistic way of getting out of this foul, decaying room. It was too risky.

    Maria is sleeping the next time Jason's heavy footsteps grow closer and he flings the basement door open. Startled from her exhausted slumber, she flies into a seated position gripping her knees close to her chest. Her heart sinks when he places yet another bag on her bed. Tentatively, she opens it, pulling out an elf costume that hums with booze. Her mind races with all the awful possibilities this costume could bring and her heart thunders in her ears.
    "Please, Jason. I have apologised to you so many times. What more can I do? You need to let me go. I am sorry for rejecting you and I am sorry I ever tried to leave you. Please, I promise I won't go to the police. I will tell everyone I ran away because I was scared of failing uni and letting people down. I will never tell anyone what happened." Maria begs with all her might.
    "It's too late. The police are already looking for you but they won't find you here. You should have thought about that before you tried to finish with me by text. I'm going to

keep you here for as long as I see fit, and when I'm done with you, I'm going to take you down to the end of my garden and set you free. I'll count to twenty and then I'll hunt you down with my rifle. It'll be my last exciting game. And when you're dead, I'll bury you so deep in my garden that no one will ever find your remains. Do you hear me?" His voice is sinister and Maria nods, tears spilling down her cheeks.

"Now get dressed."

Thirty minutes later, they park at the local shopping centre in town. Confused, Maria asks what they're doing here. Despite the embarrassment of being dressed in a child-size elf costume, a small seed of hope begins to sprout that this is her chance to get away from this monster. Surely someone will recognise her as the missing student.

Inside the shopping centre is buzzing with chatter; children cry in pushchairs and pull on their parent's arms as they beg to go into the stores enticing them with their favourite toys. Couples wander around observing window displays and discuss their shopping lists and festive plans. All the while Maria vibrates with nervous energy, praying for someone to spot her. Jason keeps his arm around her shoulder, pulling her in closer, weighing down her already weak frame. They turn the corner and a huge, snow-covered Santa's Grotto comes into view. Queuing out the door, children wait impatiently for their turn to enter. Jason lets go of Maria and whispers to her, spit coating her ear, warning her to do exactly as she has been told. She nods obediently, taking the small red sack from Jason, and approaches the end of the line.

 With as much strength as she can muster, she giggles and wishes everyone a merry Christmas. Reaching into the sack she hands the children a poorly wrapped gift, her wobbly smile faltering as the parents and children thank her. A plan starts to take shape in her mind and as she nears the grotto she decides she will run inside and beg for help, hoping someone will believe her despite her boozy scent. It has to work, someone will know she is in real danger if she tells them her name. Her heartbeat thumps behind her eyeballs as the prospect of freedom becomes tangible. As she makes it down the queue toward the grotto the children greedily rip open their presents, shrieking with disgust. Maria snaps her head towards the stunned parents and panicking children to see them holding dead rodents. A stone forms in her stomach when she sees a bloodied mouse in the palm of a young girl. One seething father storms over to her, shouting in her face about her evil act, then recoiling at the smell of her; another child's mother calls for security. Maria bursts into tears apologising profusely, desperately trying to explain that she did not know what was in the gifts, all the while Jason's roaring laughter pierces her ears.

    Screw this, she thinks. This is her chance. There is no way Jason can do anything with all these people here. Without a moment's thought, she bolts through the grotto, yanking down snowflake curtains and tripping over piles of decorative gifts. Jason's booming voice cries out behind her, yelling for her to stop. Santa and two parents huddle with a small boy as she flies past them and out the other side, knocking over a surprised elf with a sharp thud. Her throat tightens, only allowing shallow gulps of air as she races through the shopping centre. Small whimpers escape her as she powers on.

    Around the corner, the sign for the toilets comes into focus and she skids around and into the women's cubicles. Gasping for air, she grabs people's arms begging for help but they shove her away, grimacing and disgusted by the mess in front of them.

"Get out of here. You reek." An older lady in smart attire snaps.

"We don't have any change. Go on. You needn't be in here." Another chimes in. A few seconds later, most of them have cleared out, ushering their children with them and grumbling about the drunk woman. Maria cries out, begging someone to come back and help her but it is no use. She faces the mirror and tumbles back in shock as she sees her reflection for the first time in months. The bones spiking out of her face and her sunken eyes are haunting. Pale as a ghost, she stares in horror. Behind her a broad figure steps into her line of sight and her guts turn to liquid. Not a shred of hope remains and she freezes, longing for this to end but accepting her fate.

A small shooting pain in the back of her neck makes her flinch, and within seconds a drowsy numbness washes over her. Jason supports her fragile frame and guides her back to the car. Broken thoughts whirl in Maria's mind that someone must have been suspicious or reported her to the police but only time would tell. The moment the car door traps her in everything fades to black.

Maria awakes to the uneven beat of footsteps above. Her head pounds with the force of a baseball bat and the edges of her vision are blurry. It takes a few seconds to realise that the footsteps mean someone else is in the house. Despair creeps in and although she knows it is a mistake, she has to try to make her presence known. She yells for help, her voice broken and hoarse, banging her fists against the metal bed and rattling it against the wall. She cries out, begging for someone to hear and to rescue her.

A commotion above and tapping feet stop her and she listens hard to see if her plan has worked. The noises fade and the faint slam of a door has her trembling all over. Pounding footsteps descend the stairs and Jason barges into the room and backhands Maria so hard a loud crack echoes off the walls. An unearthly wail rings out as she clambers off the bed and cowers in the corner.

"You fucking whore!" Jason bellows. He closes the gap between them and swings his leg into her over and over until he's panting. When he eventually leaves, and between the blood pounding in her ears, Maria catches him muttering about her almost getting him caught.

She remains curled up, eyes squeezed shut until her entire body is rigid. Carefully, she tries to stretch out and the enormous bruises on her legs and side protest with every inch of movement. Lying down on the bed, a single tear spills down her cheek.

An uneventful few weeks pass and the bruises covering Maria's body turn a sickly yellow colour, but are fading more and more each day. Since the day of the beating, the words she overheard Jason muttering have been swirling around in her head on repeat. She had almost got their attention, almost got him caught. Still, she is stuck in this Godforsaken pit rotting away. Someone must still be looking for her, they can't have given up. This roundabout of hope and despair spins out of control daily, breaking little pieces of her heart as her hopes build and tear down again.

Lost in thought, Maria hardly notices when Jason opens the basement door and sits on the end of her bed. The bed sinks and groans under his weight and his gentle touch on her shin surprises her. Another bag rests at his feet and a calm, doting expression warms his face.

"I want you to put this on. Today will be a nice day and I want to treat you." His smooth, gravelly voice is eerie and alarms sound in Maria's head.

She looks at him quizzically. Noting her confusion, Jason explains. "I know I've been hard on you and this is an apology. I'm going to take care of you from now on. Starting tonight. I want to make you feel special because you are." His calloused fingers trace rough circles up her leg and toward her thigh. "Maria, you are my girl. I want you. Tonight is about you and me, okay?" His thumb brushes the inside of her thigh and she dies a little inside at his innuendo. He pulls out a lingerie set and holds it up to her. The frilly red lace and skimpy size makes her sick to her stomach. The bastard must be feeling lonely this Valentine's Day.

  He leaves the set on her bed and grabs her hand, guiding her up the stairs and into the bathroom, where a bubble bath steams temptingly. If it weren't for the thick coat of grease in her hair and the stale odour of vomit, ash, and sweat on her body, she would feel more dread, but she welcomes the bath like a grateful child, ashamed by her thoughts. Jason helps her into the tub and grabs a soft sponge. Swilling it below the warm water and drenching it over her delicate skin, he rubs in circles washing away the grime from the last few months. Maria relaxes into the moment, lavishing in the sensation of the torment and terror being washed away. In the back of her mind, she braces herself for his forceful hands pulling her below the surface and drowning her but Jason remains tender. Blood drains from her face as it sinks in that he is doing this so he can have sex with her. The fact that she had done it before, unaware he was such a terrible monster makes her skin crawl. She cannot face his body being close to hers or him being inside of her after all he has done. She rattles her brain for a way out of this.

Back in the basement, the grim hole smells worse than ever and the stained floor and bed make her retch as she lowers herself back down into the pit. Jason passes the lace underwear to her and she puts it on. Then he hands her what appears to be a large adult nappy.

"My darling, Cupid," Jason says, anticipating her confusion. Maria stares at him, the fear of what is to come utterly unbearable.

In the garden, the fresh winter air nips at her skin and Maria stands stiffly by a small wooden table with a bow and arrows leaning against it. In front of the remnants of the bonfire, a long bench stands with three buckets on top and cardboard cutouts of hearts.

"Take the bow and arrow and hit the buckets. Each one contains a treat for you. A real treat, I promise. Today is about us, I want it to be nice for both of us." He says. Every word sends a shiver down her spine. Apprehensively, she picks up the bow and loads an arrow with her free hand. She steadies herself, weakly drawing the bowstring. Her arm shakes at the weight of it, and before she has time to aim, the arrow shoots out, flying straight past the buckets. Facing Jason with fear in her eyes, he smiles gracefully and hands her another arrow.

Maria plants her feet firmly on the ground and aims. This time when the arrow is released it hits the very edge of the centre bucket. Jason takes the bow off her and asks her to retrieve the bucket. She complies and inside is a bottle of sparkling pink wine. Taken aback she stares at it, waiting for the other shoe to drop. Instead, Jason congratulates her and takes the wine, setting it down in the grass. He hands her the bow again and she lines up the shot. The next arrow hits the furthest bucket on the right, even though she was aiming for the left one. This bucket contains a box of heart-shaped chocolates. Dread overcomes her at the thought of being forced to consume the entire box of chocolates and a wave of nausea causes sweat to coat her upper lip. Again Jason cheers her on and encourages her to hit the final bucket. The next shot whooshes straight past the bucket and into the ground behind it, so she tries again. It takes two more attempts but she finally hits the last one. Inside is a velvet case, and when she anxiously pulls back the lid, a tennis bracelet lies delicately on the foam cushion glistening up at her. She turns to Jason, brows furrowed and blood pumping rapidly around her frozen body. His cheesy grin is a frightful sight and she instinctively retreats a step.

"I hope you like them. I want you to feel like a princess with me, Maria. You look freezing, come with me. I know what will warm you up." He says in a sickly suggestive tone. Maria follows behind, her knees wobbly and her entire body shivering, the tips of her fingers turning blue. She holds the gifts in her arms praying for inspiration to strike to save her from being forced to sleep with this disgusting creature. She contemplates pretending to faint but worries that he may just do it anyway. She looks around at the garden in the orange glow of the late afternoon light to assess a possible escape route. Despite her frozen limbs, maybe she could get far enough away to hide or run into someone. Just as the itch ignites to race away, Jason stops in his tracks and offers to help carry something for her. She hands him the chocolates and velvet box and thanks him.

Heat embraces her in a warm hug as she steps inside the farmhouse. Maria's ice-cold feet sting from the sudden rise in temperature. Jason motions for her to lead the way up the stairs, not giving her a moment to appreciate the warmth. Ascending the steps, Maria can sense his gaze on her body and can almost feel him salivating.

Just as they reach the top of the stairs, an idea springs to mind and she blindly acts on it. Maria whips around, swinging the bottle of wine as hard as she can muster into his skull. Jason staggers backwards losing his footing and rolls down to the bottom, his arms twisting at an odd angle and his eyes roll to the back of his head. Maria gasps, expecting him to jump to his feet and charge at her but he lays there, lifeless and eerily silent. Creeping down the stairs, she leaps over him and races out the front door, not stopping to look back. With every ounce of energy that remains, she puts one leg in front of the other, ignoring the biting cold and slippery ground. The winding driveway is soon in her wake. Her lungs burn as she gasps for breath on the edge of the road, debating which way to go. No cars are passing, and she can't remember which direction is the town or the village. Disoriented, she begins running left, snot coating her face as she goes and her eyes brimming with tears. Wheezing and whimpering, she pushes on until she reaches the village.

She stumbles and trips up the nearest driveway to the door and bangs on it, breathily crying out for help. Heart thundering and vision blurring, she keeps rapping on the door until a woman answers. The woman yelps in shock, then crouches to help Maria, who is kneeling on the cold patio tiles, panting and choking. Two large boots then appear in front of her face and Maria panics.

"No, no, no, no!" She cries. Two giant hands grip her under her arms and pull her inside. Sobbing, Maria fights off the man, cowering on the floor. The softly-spoken woman leans down and rubs her back. Maria flinches and apologises to the couple, recognising they are not a threat.

"Call the police, John. And ask for an ambulance too," the kind woman instructs. Maria's heart lights up, hope finally allowed to seep in.

Sometime later, the three of them are seated around the dining room table, Maria draped in a blanket. A police officer questions her about her name and family, and a paramedic checks her vitals. Maria spills a bumbling, poorly worded-account of her last few months and begs the officer to find her parents. She can't remember their numbers but the officer calmly promises to contact them. The policewoman calls into her team to request that someone find Jason and then informs them of the whereabouts of his property. With each passing minute, Maria's heart slows to a more regular beat, and a numb, empty feeling fills the cracks in her soul.

"We will take you to the hospital, and your parents can meet you there," the paramedic informs her. Maria thanks the couple and hands the blanket back.

The hospital is alive with beeping machines, talkative families visiting patients, and staff rushing from one room to another. All the commotion brings a sense of comfort to Maria as she lies in her bed hooked up to a drip of antibiotics and nourishment. The silence and stale air of the basement have been replaced with people - witnesses to her whereabouts - and the strong smell of antiseptic.

Since arriving, her body has seized up with the effort of running and months of grinding her teeth and tensing her shoulders. A woman in scrubs comes in to check on her, and as she pulls the clipboard from her bed frame, Maria asks if her parents are on their way yet. The nurse apologises as she doesn't know but she assures Maria that they will be shown straight to her once they arrive.

 Thirty minutes later, Maria is dozing, afraid to shut her eyes long enough for images to form in her mind. Flashes of the basement jolt her awake each time she drifts into a deeper sleep. The nurse she saw previously enters with a soft smile gracing her lips and informs Maria that her parents called to say they are a few minutes away. A whirlwind of emotions spreads through her body, catching in her throat. Maria sits up with her pillows propped behind her head for support and closes her eyes, imagining them walking through the door to reunite with her.

 Steady footsteps approach her bed, and the tears flooding her eyes obstruct her vision. Wiping away the salty river of built-up emotion, she is stunned into silence. The hateful face glaring back at her is contorted with rage. Frozen with shock, she is unable to move or scream or call for help. A single tinge of pain shoots up her hand, and when she looks down, Jason is withdrawing a syringe and tucks it into the pocket of his blue scrubs. Maria chokes, heart in her mouth, and pain tearing a gaping wound through her torso.

"No," she whispers, then sinks further into the mattress. Jason's sinister smile inches closer, and he places a delicate kiss on her forehead. Her eyes gradually become heavy, and she fights to keep them open, but it's too hard. Whatever Jason has injected her with is taking effect, and there is no one here to stop it. The last thing she feels is a band snuggly fit around her head.

The machines hooked up to Maria's chest rapidly begin sounding, and a doctor races into the room. He urgently begins chest compressions, ignoring or not noticing the halo placed around her head. The doctor calls for backup, and other medical staff barge in to provide aid, but it is too late. Maria's lifeless body bounces and pulses beneath them, her pain and suffering already brought to an end.

Jason slips out of the hospital ward and passes Maria's frantic parents on the way out. He rushes to their side and directs them to her room before walking away with a menacing smirk.

The Devil on the Dance Floor

The music gets worse every time I come here. It's the same churned-out electronic dance music that idiots love to blast in their car while they drive too fast through the quiet village streets in the early hours of the morning. I never went through that phase at their age. Granted, a few years ago I didn't *have* a driving licence. Nevertheless, my mind was occupied with more interesting activities, like getting laid.

The heavy beat thumps in my ears and my heartbeat matches its rhythm, stirring anxiety in my gut. If there was anywhere better to go I would, but this is the only place I've been successful in luring someone home. Tonight cannot go wrong. It's been too long since I have felt the sweet embrace of a woman, her hot breath on my ear as she screams underneath me while I pound into her. I felt good leaving the house this evening, confidence radiating from me as I sprayed my Armani, Stronger with You Intensely, Eau de Parfum. The strong amber wood and vanilla scent is perfect for the early autumn weather. Lots of women, and some men, have complimented me on it, so ten bottles of it are stocked in my bathroom cupboard, just in case it gets discontinued.

    The heat in here is stifling, the kind of humid, sweaty heat from bodies squished together as they move in time to the beat of the unbearable music. I was right to debate wearing a long-sleeve shirt; it's a shame I lost the debate and wore one anyway. Taking my hands out of my pockets, I roll up my sleeves, trying not to look like a man about to get his hands dirty. Although, that's exactly what I'm going to do. A flannel shirt was a bad choice, I look like I'm about to fix a car. It won't affect my confidence tonight though, I'm feeling good and more than ready to meet my match.

    Scanning the crowd of bodies, clashing together with their arms up and drinks swinging around in their hands, not a single woman stands out. They're all loudly screeching the words to the songs, grinding on each other, or pulling out the worst dance moves I have ever seen. Maybe this club no longer attracts beautiful, respectable women.

    The last time I was here, the dance floor was full of the most delicate, well-behaved women I have ever seen in a club. As respectable as a woman gets in a place like this. All decent women stay at home taking care of the house or spend their evenings in the gym.

It's what makes it impossible to meet anyone worthy and why I find myself taking slim pickings from these places.

    That night, those few gorgeous women danced gracefully with their friends, laughing and having a good time. And none were so stupidly drunk that they stumbled around and fell over. Of course, I was successful in picking up the most stunning, petite woman. She was obsessed with my height and pulled me over to her friends to giggle about it. Then she introduced herself and told me her name was Anna, and she was a new paralegal at a firm in town. I took a liking to her instantly. Hard-working, professional, and the most enticing pink lips I had ever seen. I told her my name was Erick - a lie - but revealing my real name was too risky. I couldn't have her telling other people about me once she got to know me. Although, if she really got to know me, she wouldn't get the chance to tell anyone anything.

    We flirted and danced all night, I bought her drinks, and with each one, she became more free-spirited and relaxed, yet remained respectable. As the night wore on she began slurring her words, which was my opportunity to head home. When I told her I was leaving, she insisted on coming with me. She had never met a more polite, handsome man, and she just had to get to know me better. I could blame it on the parfum but I know what women see in me, and I can be especially charming when I want to be. And that night, that's exactly what I wanted.

Arriving at mine, I poured her one more glass of Chardonnay and put on my well-practised fake yawn as we huddled together on the sofa. They're exceptionally easy to fake because the act of yawning triggers the reflex to do it anyway.

Anna, the sweet and gentle girl she was, took my not-so-subtle hint and led me up to my bedroom. She lay on the bed and the need in her eyes and anticipation of getting me all to herself was palpable. In her own words, she wanted to see if I was as gentle and sweet in bed as I was outside of it. My lips twitched; she was in for the best night of her life.

I lowered myself onto the bed and gently kissed her soft, supple lips. The quiet moan deep in her throat undid me. Intense heat and passion surged from within; clothes were flung off, hands scrambled for purchase wherever they could reach, and my cock throbbed with the hot-blooded need to be inside her.

When I asked if she would mind wearing a blindfold, she nodded enthusiastically.

Interesting. Anna was a dark horse. For all her innocent appearance outside, there was a devilish streak on the inside. Reaching into my drawer I retrieved the blindfold, placing it over her eyes. The excitement was almost too much, it took several deep breaths to calm myself down enough to enjoy the moment and prevent it from being over too soon. She leaned forward kissing me, missing my mouth, which caused her to giggle feverishly. Leaning over to the draw again, I took out a pair of handcuffs and placed them around the bed frame, trapping her hands above her head. Anna moaned and squirmed beneath me, unable to see what was coming next and unable to stop it. It hadn't sunk in for her yet, that her life was in my hands. In her mind, it was her pleasure in my power.

  Finally, I took the small silver pen knife from the draw and traced the blunt end up and down her stomach before inserting myself inside her and finding my rhythm. She shivered under my touch and cried out with pleasure at my length inside of her, thoroughly enjoying every second. Grunting and catching my breath, I pounded harder, dragging the knife up towards her neck where it nicked her skin and a small bead of blood trickled down onto the pillow. Anna cried out again, asking to stop and complaining that it hurt. She whined about not liking blood and it making her feel faint.

    If there is one thing that could have ruined the moment it would be the filthy whore telling me what to do. Without hesitating, I dragged the blindfold down her face and into her mouth, muffling her pathetic complaints. Her eyes widened, like a deer in headlights, tears brimming and spilling over the edges. Encouraged by her fear, I pumped harder, lavishing in the feeling of her wetness. Her legs kicked frantically behind me only driving me deeper. She screamed and writhed underneath me, almost bringing me to climax but not without me tracing the knife back down her sternum, piercing her skin several more times. Only when her voice was hoarse did I finally finish, slicing her neck as I unloaded into her. The gurgling blood spurting out of her neck matched my final pumps as I emptied my load. The euphoria had me seeing stars. The room was spinning and it took minutes before the blood rushed back to my brain and I could get up from the bed.

    After that, the sight of Anna on the blood-soaked sheets, dirtying my bedroom, and ruining the perfect atmosphere I had created made me sick. Wrapping her up in the bedding, I took her down to my basement where I dumped her in the deep hole I had dug under my house and buried her there. She'll be fine, she's not alone.

Deep in my reverie, my dick twitches as the urgency for a companion increases. A herd of screaming girls snaps me back into the present and it's hard to disguise my disgust as some drunk girls stagger past me, laughing and joking, with no regard for their ugly, unruly behaviour. Somebody needs to put them in their place. The next group to enter the dance floor instantly steals my attention. Four women face each other giggling and reaching in to shout into each other's ears over the music. A short, brunette woman with wavy hair and a simple black dress tilts her head back as she laughs at whatever her friend has just said. I'm mesmerised. She's the one. Another woman, in a denim dress, holding a tray of drinks approaches them and they each take one. They all clink glasses and cheers, and I force my eyes away in the hope that no one notices me staring. When I look back, she has her hand cupped over the top of the glass, clearly aware of her safety. I like that about her. It'll be fun to show her that no matter how safe she thinks she is, she has no control over her life and isn't safe from me. The problem with women is that they *think* they are in control. They buy rape alarms, hold their keys in between their fingers, and never walk home alone, but when a six-foot-three man with a friendly face breaks down their mental defences they don't stand a chance.

My mystery girl grabs her friend's wrist, dragging her across the dance floor and leaving the others behind. As she passes, I inhale the sweet scent of her delicious perfume. The smell of wildflowers and summer is intoxicating. Like a panther tracking its prey, my gaze follows their path to the toilet. Suddenly, a resounding thump on my shoulder knocks me backwards when I turn towards the dance floor.

"Watch it, bro. Fuck." Below me, a five-foot-nothing, broad-shouldered gym bro shouts at me. God, the urge to punch him is so strong I almost do it, but I must remind myself why I am here. *Who* I am here for.

"Sorry man. Um… Let me buy you a drink?" If being nice to this asshole is what it takes to avoid a fight then so be it.

"Hell yeah, man." The crypto idiot forcefully pats me on the back and we head to the bar. I glance over my shoulder to check if she has come out of the bathroom yet but there's no sign of her, so I impatiently push my way to the front of the bar and order two beers. It's probably best that I get one too, as I have to appear like I'm here for a night out and not just finding my next treat. The barman hands me two bottles and I tap my card on the machine to pay.

"Thanks, bro. No hard feelings, yeah?" The arrogant little man takes his beer and pushes back through the queue of people at the bar with an embarrassing amount of effort. I sigh and turn towards the dance floor again. I have found the ideal place to stand that is both inviting and innocuous. No one could accuse me of being creepy for standing a short distance from the bar, leaning on a tall table. As I reach my perfect stage-side position, the woman and her friend return from the bathroom, dancing to the dance floor.

Images of us dancing together spring to mind. I slowly walk over there and introduce myself, shaking her hand and kissing her knuckles. I pull her into my embrace, my hand resting gently on her waist and we begin turning with small steps in time to the slow beat. A slight shooting pain in my foot has us both looking down as she steps on my toes. Embarrassed for a moment, her eyes widen, but then she erupts into giggles and I join in, laughing at her two left feet. When we calm down, we dreamily look into each other's eyes and she leans in to initiate a delicate, mind-bending kiss. Suddenly, she recoils with a grimace, confesses that she has a boyfriend and apologises profusely. Rage consumes me as I grab her arm, pulling her outside and into the alley next to the club. Pinning her up against the wall, I cover her mouth with my hand, my arm on her chest to keep her in place. My other hand urgently pulls up her dress to get to her underwear.

"Hey!" *What the fuck?* I jump out of my skin as a woman appears in front of me destroying my daydream. I glare at her.

"You are so cute!" She exclaims. Her puppy dog eyes are revolting and desperate. I don't break my stare or dignify her with a response. However, I do straighten up as I realise I have been swaying to the music, deep in thought about having that woman all to myself and showing her how much she wants me. "Fine, God. There's no need to be rude." The woman shouts storming off, defeated by my lack of interest.

When I look back to the dance floor though, she's gone. Fuck. That stupid bitch distracted me. I could kill that fucking whore. If she wasn't so ugly I'd do it. Fuck. I have to find her. Frantically looking around, it's hard to see into all the dark corners of the room. The booths are full of drinkers too tired to dance, the entrance is empty, and the queue for the toilet is so long there is no way they're in there. I turn in circles, panic beginning to seep in before spotting her at the bar. My whole body relaxes and I release a breath.

Her vile friends are shouting at the bartender and it's a strain to make out what they are saying. It seems like her friend is too drunk to be served any more drinks. A few seconds later, they all stagger towards the exit, my beautiful angel at the back like a sheepdog herding her cattle. I can't let her go, so I follow behind keeping my distance.

Stepping outside, the air is cool and crisp, and the humidity of the club evaporates. I inhale a deep, clean breath, refreshing my lungs and savouring the moment. Just as I reach the end of the path leading away from the bar a huge crash has me whipping around. The shit for brains that bumped into me earlier causes a scene as he clumsily stumbles out of the bar, pushing the bouncer off him and shouting unintelligible remarks. The bumbling idiot loses his balance and hits the floor with a satisfying groan before passing out. His two friends rush to his side and slap his face trying to get him to wake up, all the while I try and fail to remove the smirk from my face. Clearly, he didn't notice the extra fizz in his drink. That's the last time the bitcoin bashing wanker will start on anyone because he can't watch where the fuck he's going.

    The girls laughing at the fool on the floor has me smiling and feeling like a champion. They head over the road towards the only other club in this tiny, derelict town. Following closely behind, I join the queue and before long, they are let in by the burly bouncer on the door. I make to go in behind them but a large hand thwacks my chest and the bouncer apologises, explaining that the venue is too full. For fucks sake. I stomp down the path towards the brewery I wouldn't usually be seen dead in. There is a huge bull's head sticker on the window with a ring through its nose and the sign reads, Bull's Head Brewery. Where they brew shitty IPAs and craft beers that taste like what I can only imagine is a replica of a peasant's piss from the 1500s. I order their most larger-like beer and sit in a window seat with a good view of the club and patiently wait. Patience hasn't always been my strong suit and it's taken many years of slow progress to reach the level I am at today. Still, it is a virtue and the best rewards are reaped from biding my time.

   Two and a half hours later the girls appear from the club and it's a relief to ditch my warm glass of bull piss and leave the bar. To no one's surprise, they head straight for the pizza place a few doors down. After some deliberation I do the same, ordering a medium margarita pizza and waiting by the door for them to prepare it. I'm famished, but not for food. My mind and dick are craving the satisfaction of this woman and having her so close to me has my senses spiralling. It's not easy to look that good under the harsh, fluorescent lights. Yet somehow, her slightly sweat-dampened hair still falls delicately around her face and her fitted dress accentuates her soft curves as she moves to sit by her friends after she finishes ordering. They're all giggling together; some look worse for wear with their hair scraped back into messy buns, eyeliner smudged, likely from throwing up, and stains on their tops from spilt drinks and god knows what else.
   The young, bearded man behind the counter calls out my order, so I collect my food and sit at the table behind them facing her. Although her friend's head is in the way as she stuffs kebab into her greedy gullet. My darling treat then gets up to grab her pizza and when

she sits back down and opens the box she lets out a thrilling moan, declaring her hunger. My pants grow tighter with every sound she makes as she takes bite after bite of pizza moaning and savouring the taste. Her friends laugh at her which is how I catch them using her name. Emily. I've not had an Emily before. She makes a joke about the pizza being better than sex. Something I can't wait to show her not to be true. I'm aching for that sultry look to be on my cock instead of her greasy, cheese pizza.

A short time later, the girls stand to leave, so I close the lid on my pizza box having only taken a few bites of one stodgy slice, and as they pass through the door behind me, I orchestrate my movements to bump into her.

"I'm sorry. I'm in your way." I say as she recoils. Our eyes meet and it takes all my effort not to grab her there and then. Her ocean-blue eyes soften as her perfect red lips curve into a smile.

"That's okay." The kindness in her eyes and her gentle tone are enough to bring me to my knees. I need her. Emily's eyes hold mine for a moment too long before she brushes past me rejoining her friends. They begin muttering between themselves; the word creep slips out a little louder, and I'm sure the crow in the denim dress intended for me to hear it. Despite my blood boiling, I mustn't hang around. I swiftly walk to my car around the corner and pull out onto the side of the road, waiting for their ride to come and take them all home. There is no way for me to know if this will work, apart from simply letting it play out. I hope to God her friends aren't staying over. I need her to go home alone. It's not the end of the world if not; it just makes it more complicated as I will have to kill them all. Though, Emily is the only one who will get to enjoy me first.

  The taxi pulls up within a few minutes and they all clamber in. At the first stop, two girls get out, shouting their goodbyes and proclaiming their love for one another. My mind is reeling with anticipation, thoughts of her body underneath me causing me to fidget in my seat.

  At the next place, Emily climbs out of the car with ease and time slows down, my heartbeat thumping in my ears as I wait for someone else to get out with her. But they don't. A cheesy, shit-eating grin spreads across my face. Emily walks briskly to the entrance of the building and does a final check of her surroundings before entering. Her obsession with safety turns me on an unhealthy amount. I turn off the engine, and when the taxi turns the corner, I leap out of the car and stealthily rush towards the apartment building. Just as I extend my arm to pull the door, it closes and latches shut. Fuck. I scramble for a way in and how to work out which apartment is hers. Then it clicks.

I walk back to the pavement and face the building, praying that luck is on my side. It is. It's hard to contain my excitement when her light comes on on the second floor and she passes by the window. I'm entranced as she reaches behind her back to unzip the dress clinging to her slight frame. I gulp as all my senses go on high alert. In slow motion, the dress drops to the floor and her figure is perfectly lit by the light inside the room, displaying her beautiful body. She bends down and when she stands back up she reaches a shirt over her head and walks away. I'm honoured that she put on a show just for me. Saliva coats my mouth and my hunger for her grows. I approach the door again and press the bell on every apartment on the third floor. A crackly voice splinters through the speakers and I explain that the apartment I need isn't answering but that I must deliver their pizza. Thankfully, they buzz me in. There is a rickety-looking lift directly ahead of me, however, I take the stairs to prologue my delicious desires. With each step that I take, I imagine her tied to her bed frame wriggling beneath me as she moans, sweeter than when she devoured her pizza.

As I near her door, a shuffling sound stops me in my tracks just out of reach of the light flooding out underneath. Then, the sound of a door closing inside and the click of a lock suggests she's in the bathroom. It hasn't occurred to me until now that she may not be alone, that she might have a roommate sleeping soundly in their room ready to ruin my night. Against my better judgment to conduct thorough research, knowing I can handle whoever is inside, I try the door handle. Inevitably, it's locked, which is no problem as I am well-versed in the art of lock picking. One of the earlier skills I learned upon finding my new hobby.

With a tremendous amount of ease, the lock snaps open and I carefully step inside, closing the door behind me without a sound. The steady rush of the shower and steam seeping out from under the door confirms Emily is nicely distracted in the shower, so I take the opportunity to look around.

On the right is the kitchen and it's

immaculate, not an item out of place. There are dishes stacked neatly to dry by the sink and the table is set with matching placemats and coasters, although it is too dark to see the pattern. There are fresh flowers on the windowsill and a faint fragrant smell permeating from them. It's not a pleasant smell but the flowers are pretty enough. Leaving the kitchen, I pass a closed door. For fear that it could be Emily's roommate, I don't look inside and hope they sleep like the dead. The next room along is Emily's bedroom; it is immediately clear as there are large grey letters hung on the wall spelling her name. Underneath are Polaroids and pictures of her with friends and travelling.

The shower shuts off and in a haste to remain hidden, I squeeze myself into her built-in wardrobe. The scent of her clothes invades my senses, making my head spin. God, she smells good.

A while later, Emily enters the room, turning off the main light and putting a small bedside lamp on. Watching through the slight crack in the door, she removes the towel wrapped around her head and brushes her hair in long, delicate strokes. Then she weaves it into two neat French braids and climbs into bed. The air is stuffy in here and my throat feels like sandpaper. The sensation is urging me to cough and clear my throat. I suppress the feeling the best I can.

    Emily leans over to turn off her lamp getting comfortable in bed. However, she immediately picks up her phone, the soft blue light illuminating her face. This is my chance. The light in her eyes will prevent her from seeing me and I'm light enough on my feet that she won't hear me over the videos of tonight that she is watching. Carefully, I nudge the door open just enough to step out of the closet, pausing immediately to judge her reaction. When she doesn't look up from her phone I creep closer, holding my breath, barely blinking. My eyes have had time to adjust to the dark so I can see clearly enough where I am stepping, although my gaze is fixed firmly on Emily. Her innocence is evident now she is tucked into her bed, with an oversized shirt on, and plaited hair framing her face to display her young features.

    An alarming creak sounds below me as I take my next step. Hitching my breath, I pause, waiting for all hell to break loose. But the fearful shrieks don't come. For a second I hesitate wondering if she knows I'm here and is ignoring me for some reason. That's impossible though, no one in their right mind would be this calm with an intruder in their home. Emily locks her phone and rolls over in bed to face away from me, confirming that she must not know that I'm here.

    I inch closer, my hunger ready to be satiated, ready to devour this beautiful woman and bring her to sweet salvation while she screams before the light leaves her eyes. As I loom over her petite frame, claws ready and jeans bulging, searing pain spikes through my thigh. My head snaps down and the dull outline of a knife protruding from my femur has my vision blurring. A gasp is all I can manage as I lock eyes with the devil whore leaping up from the bed. Fumbling backwards, my leg throbs with every step, the knife wriggling and burning in my flesh. The little bitch shoves my chest with all her might and I topple backwards trying to gain purchase on anything on my descent to the floor. The curtain tears and rips from the wall as it is not enough to support my weight. Then, an almighty crack rings through my skull when I clash with the edge of the wooden desk and darkness descends.

    A dull throb pulses through my temples and behind my eyes. Instinctively, I attempt to reach for the back of my head to feel the wound and assess the damage. Realisation slowly seeps in as I wiggle my arms that they are tied behind my back with a cable. Despite the intense pain pounding in my brain, I gradually force open my eyes, only to be met with Emily's arrogant smirk looking back at me.

"You bitch." I spit at her feet, desperately trying to move my legs. The pain in my bleeding thigh is excruciating. I end up awkwardly on my back crushing my hands. I curse and writhe about until I am half-seated against the wall. Crinkling underneath me snatches my attention and my heart rate spikes involuntarily when I notice I am sitting on plastic sheets. It's okay, I will get out of these binds and rip her goddamn head off. She doesn't know who she's messing with.

"You know, I can shout and someone will come to your door and see what you've done," I snarl.

"Oh honey, no. They won't. This bad boy is as soundproof as it gets." She bangs on the wall with her fist and the dull sound it makes proves her point.

"I'm going to kill you and it's going to be so fucking good to watch you bleed out," I growl.

"That's where you're wrong. Don't you want to hear about how I caught you?" Her voice is so sickly sweet and it grinds my teeth.

"Enlighten me," I grit out.

"Oh good, story time. You see, I was Anna's friend. You might remember her, small and cute as a button. A lot like me in some ways, but not at all in others. She was so smart and capable, witty and generous, but you wouldn't know that. Because all you were interested in was feeding your sick fantasies." I grin up at her, reminiscing on that wonderful night. No matter what she does to me, she will always know that I took her friend's life. Emily narrows her eyes, a silent gesture that lets me know she understands what I'm thinking about.

"Your pupils are dilating just thinking about it, you rotten freak. It's okay though, because after tonight, you'll have a taste of what she went through and when you burn in hell you'll have the scars to remember it." Her grin is threatening and a bead of sweat exposes my rising panic.

"What you don't know about Anna, is that she sent me her location when she got to your house, so I knew exactly where she was before she went missing. Now, you may have thought you were clever turning her phone off the second you were done with her, but it was already too late. She asked me to pick her up because she didn't want to stay the night. She must have known deep down that you were a pig, she was just too caught up in your fake charm to see it. So, I drove to your place and waited outside in the car for her. Only I heard something extremely troubling, a scream sounding less like pleasure and more like fear. When I called her, she didn't pick up, so I took that as my cue to investigate. Nothing happened for a while as I checked through your living room window. So, I went around the back hoping to get a better view through the kitchen. It was then that I saw you plodding into the room carrying a duvet. Anyone glancing at this might have thought you were doing your washing in the middle of the night, weird but believable. However, the two small feet poking out the end gave you away. At first, I panicked, dialled the police and crouched down hoping to God you didn't see me. But before the call handler on the other end could answer I hung up. I knew in my heart that *I* wanted to be the one to get revenge. It could have been adrenaline or fear that aided my decision, but the morning after, once my heartbeat had settled and I finally ran out of tears, I knew that justice in the shape of you going to prison wasn't going to be enough. It wouldn't cut it. You deserved so much worse. And I was going to be the one to give it to you."

"You're insane and just as bad as me if you do this," I grunt, desperation clawing at my insides. My mind is racing a mile a minute trying to find a means to escape. The dull ache in my head is clouding my judgement and it's impossible to focus.

"You would think that. Except I don't. Because after that night, I started researching missing girls in the area and a pattern emerged. Five missing girls in the space of two years. Now I would bet my life savings on where they might be." She chuckles slightly, and then anger sets in contorting her face, darkening her eyes.

"So, I'm doing this, not just for Anna, but for all of them. They all deserve equal justice. An eye for an eye, if you will. You're just lucky there's only one of you. But I will drag this out long enough for you to suffer enough for all of them." Reaching behind her, she pulls out a huge carving knife, specifically designed to cut meat. I swallow the bile rising in my throat. The edges of my vision are closing in, dizziness descending on me from the loss of blood from my leg wound. I have nothing to say. There is nothing I can say that will change her mind or make this any more swift. This stupid bitch tricked me and now I'm tied up and defenceless. She looked so innocent, an easy unknowing prey. And now, here I am, life on the line and no foreseeable way out.

"Watching you plan your way out of this is wildly entertaining. I may let you plot a little longer but first I want to tell you how I caught you."

"It's fucking obvious how you caught me you crazy bitch." She laughs and it grates on my soul. I thrash violently on the floor and try using the wall to get to my feet. From the chair opposite me, Emily swipes her legs out with such force that I come crashing down in an instant, landing on my arms and grumbling in agony.

"There, there. Hush now, there isn't much left to the story." She twists the point of the knife into the tip of her finger until a spot of blood drips down the blade. Her eyes twinkle in unison with the reflection of the blade.

"You were much easier to reel in than I anticipated. I sat outside of your house in my car and tracked your movements. You're not very aware of your surroundings for someone with so much to hide. It was very quickly apparent that you liked to hunt at night and so I followed you to a bar and watched you watch them, your trousers getting tight at every woman you found attractive. It was pathetic really. One thing was clear though, you liked short, brunette women. Funnily enough, my natural hair is blonde, but I dyed it just for you. You can thank me later. The rest was easy. I knew you couldn't resist me in a little black dress. Then I just needed to keep my distance so that you couldn't get close enough to me to try and lure me back to your place. Except, I had to be irresistible enough that you were compelled to follow me home instead. Which is exactly what you did. I knew you'd find a way inside once you had the right motivation. Cue my little show. I already had the knife under my pillow and the cameras I set up in my apartment showed me everything you were doing while I was *in the shower*. And you know the rest." Standing from the chair she towers over me, the knife glistening under the dim lights above. Bending to meet my eyes, she smears the blood from her finger down my cheek and cups my chin. Snarling, I pull away but there is no use. There is nowhere to go, my energy is depleting and my hands are tied. Literally.

"You don't know what it's like to kill someone. You have to live with it for the rest of your life. It will drive you mad to have my blood on your hands. You'll see it everywhere and my face will haunt your dreams. You will never get one good night of sleep." I don't know that to be true, as I sleep better than ever after a kill but I am desperate for her to change her mind and to turn me into the police. I'd be delusional to think she'd let me go.

"You sweet, sweet idiot. I will finally rest peacefully knowing you are no longer here to prey on defenceless women, and each night a smile will grace my lips knowing I was the one to stop you."

She kneels, bringing the knife to my chin and nicks the skin. Warm blood pools and drips down my neck. I gulp, bracing myself for what's to come.

Coming for Me

A dull ache pulses up my arm as I lean against the dining table with the house phone still clutched to my ear. I carefully place the phone down on the table with a sigh. I've lost count of how many times I have called the police in the last six months, and yet, they have no interest in helping me. I'm sick of hearing them tell me there's nothing they can do, and I'm even more fed up that every time they do send someone, the sick bastard has fled the scene.

Eyeing the window above the kitchen sink, the only thing visible is the dull reflection of the room in the black glass. With a huff, I get up and put away the remaining leftovers from dinner, then retrieve a painkiller from the cupboard and swill it down with the last of my water. Closing the cupboard door a flicker of light reflects on the gloss cabinet. Whooshing around to investigate, I lean over the sink and strain to see into the garden lit by the outdoor light that is triggered by movement. Staring intensely, I am startled when a fox races across the grass and into the bushes. Goosebumps spread up my arms and the back of my neck as I clutch my aching chest. Another flash of movement snatches my attention in the far bushes. I observe the dark corners of the garden waiting to catch a glimpse of something, *anything*, but nothing comes. A few minutes go by and I give up, retreating to the living room, heartbeat still fluttering.

A home should feel safe like a sanctuary to rest and recharge between busy days of work and life's never-ending to-do lists. Yet, since my husband left me eight months ago, I have been terrorised by this creep who must know I am now living on my own. It was slow in the beginning, almost undetectable. The odd knock on my door that when I answered revealed nobody to be there, or the occasional time the light in the back garden came on for no apparent reason. I thought nothing of it at first. Even when I would get random calls on my home phone and upon answering, all I could hear was breathing on the other end. I naively put it down to children playing silly pranks, not knowing they were bothering a grieving woman. Around a month went by with the calls becoming more frequent, though the raspy breathing remained the same. Until one day the calls stopped. Two days went by with nothing and the relief was palpable. For the first time in over thirty days, my shoulders relaxed and my jaw unclenched. It didn't last long though. One evening, bin bag in hand ready to take outside, I froze on the spot. A tall silhouette appeared in the far corner of my back garden in a horrifying tableau. Everything in my gut screamed danger and I dropped the bag and immediately called the police. By the time they arrived, the figure had disappeared into the darkness. The police thoroughly checked the premises, but with nothing more to go on than the ghostly figure that I described, there was nothing they could do. And on it went for the next month. On random evenings, this unnerving statue would appear in my garden, always too far away for me to make out his features but close enough to see that he was facing me. I could feel his penetrating gaze and it caused my hair to stand on end.

And so began the numerous calls to police, but it was useless. They never found the perpetrator. Night after night, I lay awake in bed, tired to the bone, yet too scared to shut my eyes long enough for sleep to take hold. Eventually, it was affecting my work and I missed the deadline for two reports. My boss called me in and told me that although he understood I was going through a hard time without my husband, I could not let it continue to affect my job. Too embarrassed to lay on more personal issues and in need of one place where I could be treated normally, I gave him my word that I'd pick myself up and do better.

    That night, I took a couple of over-the-counter sleeping pills to help and they worked. I woke up the next day feeling much more refreshed. It wasn't until I got in the shower, that I noticed some small bruises on my legs that I had no recollection of getting. I didn't dwell on it though, as I got to work and did more that day than I had in months. My colleagues complimented my bright complexion and newfound motivation, and I left work feeling much more optimistic.

    From that day, I successfully managed to compartmentalise my life. At work, I thrived and proactively met all my targets and got back on track with my boss; and at home, I allowed myself to be a bundle of nerves and to face my issues alone.

    Despite calling the police tonight, I can still sense the man haunting my garden, watching me. Only right now, I can't see him. The fox is likely long gone, on the hunt for food. Yet, the outside light came on again as I entered the kitchen to wash my glass in the sink before going to bed. Curiously, I turn the tap off and lean forward again to try and spot the reason for the light being triggered, but again there is nothing. Giving up, I resume washing my glass.

    Just as I finish cleaning the remaining pots, the outside light turns off and my blurry reflection stares back at me. Something feels off and all my nerves tense. I look harder, trying to see past the reflection when two sinister glowing eyes appear inches from the glass. I leap back in horror, dropping a plate on the floor which shatters at my feet. Blood pumping, I scramble and shuffle, unsure what to do, when the adrenaline surging through my veins has me acting before thinking. Lurching forward, banging on the window, I search for his eyes or stalking figure but he has already gone.

    "I'm imagining it. There is no one there." I mutter to myself.

    As my adrenaline dips, a shooting pain begins in the ball of my foot. Looking down, blood is smeared across the marble-tiled floor and over the shards of porcelain. I hobble backwards and into a chair, off my wobbly legs. I pull my foot onto my knee to assess the wound and luckily only a few small cuts are visible. Taking a deep steadying breath, I check to see that the backdoor is locked and confirm I am safely barricaded inside. Desperation gnaws at my gut, and pushing my conflicted feelings aside, there is only one person I can think to call for help. I hope my husband will offer to come and check that whoever is in my garden is gone. The phone trills and trills until it eventually goes to voicemail. It's past midnight, so he must be asleep.

Once my blood pressure has lowered enough for my heart to stop hammering in my chest, I clear the broken plate and then clean and dress my foot.

In bed, I lay staring at the ceiling, too afraid to close my eyes and on high alert for any noises or signs that the creep is out there. My heart rate thumps steadily against my ribcage, and my limbs tingle in readiness to flee. I cradle my wrist to my chest, pondering over how I managed to injure it overnight. It must be from carrying all my shopping bags in one trip from the car. That's the only slightly strenuous thing I have done recently.

Hours pass agonisingly slowly until the tablets take effect. The first peak of the morning light is a blessing. The low buzz of traffic from cars commuting to work and kids walking to school brings a sense of security that doesn't exist after dark. I sluggishly drag myself to the bathroom to get ready.

In the office surrounded by people, the hum of day-to-day activity, urgent meetings, and back-to-back calls, I regain my composure. On my way home I feel a little more at ease and the frightful experience of the previous night doesn't seem so dramatic. In fact, by the time I finish my evening meal and the outside light hasn't been triggered once, I'm almost convinced that I have imagined the whole thing. That is until I plonk myself down on the sofa and turn on the television. Halfway through the romantic film I put on to lighten my mood a shadow forms against the curtains. Fear envelops me as my eyes lock in on the unwavering form. It perfectly matches the shape I have seen in my back garden many times. Grabbing my phone from the arm of the chair, I swiftly call my husband, barely blinking.

"Come on. Pick up, pick up, pick up." The phone rings out again, going to voicemail. This time I decide to leave one.

"Hey, it's just me. Sorry to call you so late again. I hope I'm not interrupting, it's just… well I think there's someone outside my house and I don't know what to do. Please can you come over? I daren't go out and see what it is. Sorry if this wakes you." The words spill out in a trembling heap.

Alone and afraid, I push any feelings of embarrassment about calling the police again aside. The operator answers and I explain the situation, recounting the previous calls to report the same man stalking me. Though, while I am sharing my concerns with the operator, the figure retreats out of sight and I know in my gut that if the police conduct a check they will find nothing. So, although defeated, I tell the man on the other end of the phone to log the report but assure him that I don't need someone to come to my house.

After hanging up, the anxiety and strain of it all is too much. I weep uncontrollably into the cushion resting on my lap. Tears seep into the soft fabric as the weight of it all bubbles over the surface needing to escape.

A firm knock on the front door scares me stiff. I wait with bated breath for any sound, hoping to shortly hear footsteps moving away from my house. Another knock follows suit and I jump to my feet contemplating hiding upstairs. However, the voice accompanying the second knock is a relief to hear. It's a policewoman announcing her presence. I rush to the door and peek through the peephole, thankful to see a uniformed officer on the other side. I open the door, keeping the metal latch on, and the woman explains that she is doing a wellness check and asks for permission to head around to the back garden. I agree and briefly divulge what has been happening.

The policewoman assesses the areas all around the house and checks the doors are locked and windows are inaccessible from the outside. Once she is satisfied that I am safe, she comes back to the front door where I am waiting.

"There are no signs that anyone was here. The plant beds don't seem disturbed and all your windows and doors are secure. You may want to consider installing cameras. It might help you to feel safer," she suggests.

"Thank you, I will do that. I appreciate you coming here."

Regardless of the officer's visit, the anxiety is hard to shake off, so I make a lavender tea and take a couple more sleeping pills in the hopes of making it through the night with some sleep. To help make the bedroom feel a little safer, I barricade the door with my dresser and wedge it under the handle. If I need to use the bathroom, I will have to hold it until morning. In bed, it helps to know that my room is more secure and for the first time in a while, I fall asleep before midnight.

When I wake up, the lamp next to my bed

is lying on its side and bits of glass from the shattered bulb are spread across the floor. My stomach drops because I have no recollection of doing it and it didn't wake me up. I shuffle across the bed and lean over the edge to assess what might have happened but nothing becomes obvious. I get out of bed from the other side and when I pass my tall mirror I have to do a double take. A long, reddish scrape goes down the full length of my arm. I get closer to the mirror, pulling at my arm to get a better view of it and rattle my brain about how I have yet another injury. Then, in the corner of my eye, I notice the marks on the floor where the dresser was before I moved it and it occurs to me that it could have happened when I shoved it in front of the door. It doesn't explain why it looks so fresh but I could have agitated it in the night.

  After breakfast, I call a few security companies and settle on a quote for cameras in the front and back garden, offering to pay extra if they can squeeze me in as soon as possible, and they agree to come the following day. Despite spending my morning at work focused on out-of-work issues, the rest of the day is productive and it feels like things are starting to get better.

When I get home after work, a weight has been lifted. Knowing that tomorrow my house will be more secure, I am confident I can make it through one more night. Kicking off my shoes in the doorway, I drop my bag and head to the kitchen for a long-awaited cup of tea. Immediately something feels off. A shiver runs through me as I glare at the glass on the table. The same glass that I am confident I washed and put away this morning. Shakily, I put it in the sink, rewinding my brain to retrace my steps. The more I think about it the foggier my brain becomes. My morning routine is so deeply embedded that I can't remember specifically doing it today over any other day. Maybe if I act like I remember not putting the glass away, I will believe it. This morning must have been a rush or I could have been preoccupied with ordering the cameras. I flick the kettle on and attempt to put it out of my mind.

For dinner, I prepare spaghetti bolognese and put the extra portions into Tupperware to eat over the next few days. As I am wiping down the countertops a rustling sound upstairs shakes me to my core. Like a deer in headlights, I go rigid, straining to hear for another sign that there is something upstairs, but I don't hear anything. Already desperate to put my lounge-ware on and against my better judgment, I go upstairs to investigate. It's silly to jump out of my skin at every little sound; all houses creak and groan as they heat up and cool down.

As I carefully ascend the stairs, creeping one step at a time, the rustling sounds again. Weak at the knees and head screaming to run, I keep going, determined to face whatever is up there. I pause at the top of the stairs, listening for any signs of danger, when a crash of toppled-over bottles erupts in the bathroom. I jerk backwards in shock bracing myself against the wall.

"Just breathe. It's fine." I whisper. "Go on."

After a long calming breath, I inch towards the bathroom, peering into my bedroom briefly as I pass to ensure it is empty of intruders. When I get close enough, I gently nudge the door with the tip of my fingers. Time passes in one long drawn-out moment, silence filling the air. Then all of a sudden, a huge grey beast flaps around frantically. I shriek, then jump into action, scooping up the flustered pigeon and guiding it out the window. Sharing the same ruffled feeling as the bird, I giggle at the stupidity of it all.

Washing my hands, I let the cool water steady my focus, when my heart sinks to my feet. I am absolutely certain I did not leave that window open. It is a rare occurrence that after a morning shower, I will open the window to let the fresh air in and I am positive today is not one of those days. Dread sits like a stone in my stomach as I wrack my brain trying to recount my morning. It all feels so foggy and unclear. Failing to piece together what I did and didn't do before leaving for work, I put it down to the stress of being terrorised by this faceless man for the last few weeks.

Too afraid to feel comfortable in my living room and in desperate need of a good night's sleep, I settle into bed early. It soon becomes clear that sleep will not be possible without a little help, so I take a couple more sleeping pills and try to relax as they take effect.

In the morning, after tossing and turning all night managing only short bursts of fitful sleep, I wait patiently for the security company to arrive and fit the cameras. The lovely gentleman thoroughly explains how to operate the system and ensures it is working and connected to my phone. He leaves me with a newfound sense of calm knowing I can show police this mystery man if he appears again.

I shower to wash off the cold sweat from the night before, and under the scalding hot water, a dull throbbing pain forms beneath my left shoulder. When I finish my shower, I twist at odd angles in the mirror trying to get a look at my back. A deep purple bruise the size of my fist sits just under my shoulder blade. How the hell has that happened? I've never seen a bruise that angry before, much less on my body. I must have done it thrashing around trying to get rid of the bird. I didn't feel it at the time but it could have been the adrenaline. I turn some more, reaching my arm around to press the tender spot. It immediately aches and I roll my shoulders a few times to relieve some tension before getting dressed.

    The rest of the day is more relaxing, as I find a cosy spot on the sofa and read a book. The stress of the last couple of months has left my body limp with exhaustion that has caught up to me now that I am finally able to feel safe in my home. Not wanting to expend too much energy, I put in a frozen pepperoni pizza for dinner and pour myself a large glass of white wine to settle the last of my spent nerves. Taking a long swill of wine, my stomach warms with the sharp taste of citrus and crisp apple. Savouring the acidic sensation on my tastebuds, I exhale a sigh of relief.

    Although, the feeling is instantly replaced with fright as a sudden golden glow flickers in my peripheral vision. Turning slowly to face the window, tears fill my eyes in frustration at my immediate terror. The absence of a fox trotting along the grass and the looming figure leaning against the rotten apple tree confirm my fears. Scrambling for my phone, there is no notification from the camera. Nervous rage boils my insides at my inability to use technology. I call my husband; all the while my eyes remain fixed on the malevolent shadow. Despite the last encounter with my husband ending on tense terms, I cannot understand his lack of response to my pleas for help. I do not believe that things have grown that sour, and as much as I need him right now, I desperately wish to mend the broken bridges between us.

    A swell of sadness overwhelms me in an oil spill of mingling emotions. Drying my eyes, I fix my sight on the apple tree, my heart sinking when I realise the man has gone. I contact the police again, begging them to come, explain that I did what they said and have a camera but I think he is standing out of range. The operator informs me that they will look into sending someone but that I should call back if the camera picks him up. Frustrated, I huff and groan, pacing back and forth through the kitchen like a caged animal, when in the middle of my garden he appears clear as day in the copper light. His forbidding face peers eerily back at me with a deathly calm expression. He's freakishly still and his messy unkempt hair spikes on end like he has been rolling around on the ground or hiding in bushes. I scream at the top of my lungs, then race out of the kitchen and upstairs, stumbling up each step in my rush to safety. Trembling like a leaf, I cower in the corner of my bedroom praying for someone to help me. Thoughts of being murdered in the one place I should feel safe spiral out of control and all the ways he could harm me has me sobbing uncontrollably. Wet snot drips to my upper lip and tears pour down my ghostly white cheeks as I rock gently on the floor.

"Someone will come. The police will come," I mumble.

A loud knock at the door threatens my heart to give out but I don't dare to leave my room or check the cameras in case the man is still there in plain view. I figure if it is the police they will at least scare the intruder away. For the next few hours, I sit tightly hugging my knees and too afraid to move or check my phone.

The next day at work, I am dog tired. My

greasy hair is slicked back into a tight bun and I have made no effort to look presentable as I drag myself into the office. A coworker, who has known me for many years, approaches me twice to ask if I am ok, and both times I shrug them off and disclose that I have not been sleeping well, but refuse to elaborate any further. My colleague offers me a coffee and relays that she is always available for a chat if I need it but I thank her and make an excuse to leave early, claiming that I feel unwell.

Leaving the office building, I head straight to my car, checking my surroundings for anything weird or off, in case the mystery man is watching me outside of my home as well. After thoroughly scanning in all directions there is nothing obvious and no suspicious-looking people that catch my attention. However, when I near my car there is a note placed under my window wiper. My heart skips a beat and I instinctively look around again to ensure no one is watching me and grab the note. Feeling too vulnerable to stand here and read it, I shove it in my bag and rush home.

Safely inside, I take out the note and laugh a little manically because it is just an advert for a car wash service near the office.

"Oh my god. You're losing it," I say,

hysterically.

The lack of sleep and the constant hounding of my nervous system in the last few months has finally reached its breaking point and I fall into a deep, dreamless sleep on the sofa for the remainder of the afternoon. When I wake it's dark inside and out, so I leap up to turn on the lights, with that sixth sense that I am not alone like the one I got as a teenager turning the light off and running upstairs. Yawning and trudging to the kitchen, I pull the blind down in the window so I don't have to look outside.

Having caught up on some sleep, a calmer more logical mindset has taken hold and the events of the last few days seem a lot smaller. There has to be an explanation for this and I will get to the bottom of it. Feeling a lot more perky, I call my mother and invite her here for dinner. I am unsure whether to tell her what has been happening. I just know that I want to have some light conversation after such a rough few days.

By the time we finish dinner the world seems so much brighter. With a lightness in my step, I load a tray with tea and biscuits to carry to the living room. But when I lift it, shooting pains surge up my arm and I drop it onto the counter, spilling the tea.

"Goodness, are you okay, Sarah?" My mother asks when I yelp.

"I'm fine. I've just hurt my wrist a bit," I tell her.

"How have you done that?" she asks, cleaning the mess and making fresh cups of tea.

"I honestly don't know. I just woke up one morning and it felt really sore," I confess. She gives me the usual motherly medical advice to rest it and use heat and then heads to the living room. It's getting late and I want to make sure I can sleep, so I take a sleeping tablet now to give it time to kick in for when my mum leaves. I join her and we sink into the sofa to talk about nothing in particular.

An hour goes by and it starts to get late, around the time I usually get a fright. The routine of being stalked has caused my body to react in preparation for seeing something terrifying. I am bracing myself for danger.

Tentatively, I wait and minutes go by with no sign of anyone outside, no lingering shadows, and no spine-tingling sense that I am being watched. All the while, my mother finishes the dregs of her tea and is reeling off the rest of her plans for the week. A peculiar sense of calm washes over me and I wonder if the whole thing is in my mind and if I have imagined it all. But then the image of the dishevelled man locking eyes with me the night before sends goosebumps across my body.

"Are you alright, my love?" My mother asks.

"Oh yes, it's just dropping a bit colder in the evenings now. I'll be putting the heating on soon," I lie.

"It is getting nippy out there now. I suppose I better be going home. Thank you for dinner, it was lovely and so nice to see you looking more yourself." My mother coos, stroking my face and then embraces me in a hug.

At the door, we hug one final time and I tell my mother to drive safely. I watch her walk to the street towards her car and then shut the front door. Before I can lock it, a tapping sound grabs my attention. Throat in my mouth, I know instantly where it is coming from, and I speed to the kitchen to pull up the blind and search the garden. There is nothing out there, and just as I lower the blind again, the tapping sounds from the living room window. Hurtling into the room, I draw back the curtain and stagger back. He's there, waving at me like a creepy clown in a haunted fairground.

It suddenly clicks that the door is unlocked and my mother is outside getting to her car. An almighty rage boils over and with steam puffing out of my ears, I storm outside ready to face whoever this menacing stalker is, if not to protect my mum, who he must have been watching leave the house, then to put an end to this once and for all. The last few months of terror, head-spinning madness and feeling like my life is in constant danger, erupt in a frenzy of anger. Screaming at him to leave me alone and to stop tormenting me, I wave my arms around attacking the stranger. The more I let it out, the more infuriated I get.

Then, two hands claw and grab me trying to pull my attention to them. A distant voice echoes around me slowly coming into focus. When I tune into the panic-stricken woman next to me, I halt immediately. Eyes wide and frantically looking around for the man I was just fighting, I begin to hyperventilate. A wave of pain and anguish comes crashing down over my weak, defeated body and I crumble to the ground as the strength in my legs diminishes.

My heart cannot take this level of hurt. Each shred of tissue is being torn away and burned into ash. My mother kneels behind me, arms enveloping me in a protective, gut-wrenching hug and I flinch at the pressure on my bruised back. My mum recoils and then gently pulls down my top to reveal the nasty mark.

"My God, Sarah. What happened?" Her voice cracks and it breaks my heart into tiny shards.

"He's everywhere, mum. He won't leave. I can't sleep with him there," I bawl.

"It's okay, darling. He's gone. He's not here anymore." My mother repeats. I heave and sob, unable to take a full breath because the reality is all too much.

"He's gone, my love. You know that. He's not coming back." My mother says, shakily.

"I know, mum. But I miss him. And I will never be able to make things right. We shouldn't have left it like that," I weep between breaths.

"I know, love. But one argument isn't everything. Your relationship was so much more than that. Let's get you inside." She helps me to my feet, rubbing my back and gripping my arm for support.

Back in the living room, I gradually begin to calm down.

"I've not been sleeping well and I think it's made me lose my head a little," I admit.

"It seems like more than that, Sarah. Where

are these injuries coming from?" I instinctively rub my arm and roll my shoulder, the pain coming back into focus.

"I honestly don't know. I've been taking sleeping pills and they put me in such a deep sleep and when I wake up I have a new bruise or mark. I'm probably just sleepwalking, right? What I'm seeing isn't real, it's not him?" I'm going crazy. I've been going mad for months and it's suddenly just dawned on me that I'm the reason for it. I shouldn't need confirmation that he's not here but I need her to tell me I'm not insane.

"Honey, you shouldn't take those for long periods of time. Try to come off them and see how you go. You're not crazy, you're grieving." A new wave of heartbreak washes over me.

"Your husband loved you so much, Sarah. And if he were here now, he would tell you that. He knows how much you loved him too. You can't let your argument and silly break haunt you. It will eat you alive when you have all these good memories to focus on. Sarah, you need to grieve for Craig but you don't need to beat yourself up. Protect his memory, and honour him and yourself by celebrating his life," my mum soothes.

"I know, mum. It's just been so hard." I lay down on the sofa, closing my eyes and my

mum sits next to me gently stroking my hair.
"I know, love."

Risky Research

12th February 2008

I apologise in advance for my jumbled thoughts. I must write this down before it is too late.

Tears sting my eyes as I put pen to paper, exhaustion weighing heavy on my eyelids. Still, sleep evades me. Every evening when the sun sets below the horizon, it starts. The knocks at the bedroom window, the echoes of my name being called down the chimney, and when I wake, the bloody handprints on my front door. Great cracks have split through my hands as the continuous use of bleach has burned my skin in my attempt to remove the blood. So much blood.

There is something I must confess. But before I do you must believe me, I am saving lives. There is no other choice but to get to the bottom of this. No matter what.

You see, I am a doctor, and I have performed many surgeries in my twenty-nine and three-quarter years as one. Particularly on the brain. Only now, I fear I am going mad. My once steady hands tremble with worry. Growing more unsteady as each dreadful day passes.

If you are reading this, then the worst has happened, or at least the worst that I can picture while I still possess a shred of sanity. If all that is lost, then maybe you are reading this and I am still here. Only it is just my body, and my mind is lost to whatever it is that is haunting me.

You may be thinking, haunting? What did you do? Everybody makes mistakes, you must simply learn from it, and move on. To let it haunt you will cause you to be distracted and lead to more mistakes, or will ruin your confidence and get in the way of all the good you can do. You're right. However, that is not the type of haunting I speak of. For this, is the unexplainable kind, the supernatural kind. I know, a doctor who believes in the supernatural, maybe I am losing my mind. Nonetheless, there is something otherworldly going on and I am the target of it.

It all started six months ago. On a cool, chilly night in December on my journey back from London. As I stepped off the train at Manchester Piccadilly station, a man approached me. He was unusually tall and his slim frame only accentuated his looming figure. He wore a long, black trench coat and pointed leather boots with a small heel. An amusing costume. At first, he smiled gently, his hazel, cat-like eyes glowing under the harsh platform lights. Then, he stopped a respectable distance away.

I am always careful of my surroundings, I know there are dangers out there every woman must remain on high alert for. But sometimes you just get a feeling about people, a familiarity even though you have never met before. This man, I knew, was kind. I said hello and he asked me for directions in this smooth, crisp voice. You could almost drink it, it was intoxicating.

Unfortunately, the place this mystery man was seeking was not somewhere I was familiar with and so I explained that I could not help him as my phone had died during my lengthy journey. And so, he thanked me and went on his way. It wasn't until I left the station that I remembered the place he was referring to. The Midnight Bar was located near the old church and graveyard. I hastily spun around and headed back to see if he was still there, but there was no sign of him, on the platform or in the entrance to the station. Mind you, it was the middle of the night and the station was relatively empty, so a man of his height should have stuck out like a sore thumb. Nevertheless, I figured he found his way or left the station to try and find someone who could help him.

Moments later, I resumed my journey home, forgetting all about the lost peculiar man. But wouldn't you know it, as I am rounding the corner *to Belvoir Street, he comes hurtling into me, not looking where he is going. I've never been one for clumsiness, it could be life-threatening in my occupation, yet the look on his face was disarming. His startled eyes and furrowed brows had me forgiving his misstep in a second. We both chuckled, sending clouds of condensation puffing out into the open. What a coincidence, I thought, and explained that he needed to find the church and graveyard not far away and the bar would be neatly tucked behind it. It occurred to me to show him the way, since it was not so far from my house. In the end, I felt safer to provide more accurate directions and be on my way. After all, if you can't listen to your gut then you're as good as deaf.*

The mysterious man thanked me profusely and disappeared into the shadows. But before I could even round the corner, stars and the night sky swirled all around. By the time my eyeballs caught up with me, I was anchored to the floor, staring up into the dead of night. The man kneeling over the top of me grunted and drooled as he reached for my handbag. My grip tightened and I shrieked and yelled until he began to panic, eyes darting around to check for onlookers. I clawed and scratched until suddenly the enormous weight lifted and the disgusting thief shouldered the floor next to me, groaning loudly. A charcoal black leather boot stepped into my line of sight and a hand extended down to help me to my feet.

We each leaned against the wall catching our breath. He must have run over as soon as he heard me yelling. What a gentleman. My knight in shining armour. Although, a sudden and entirely rational desire to be at home had me bumbling my thanks and stumbling away, gripping onto the wall for support. My knees were like jelly and my head throbbed from the impact of the tackle to the ground.

A few shuffles of my feet later, the honourable man offered to guide me home safely, and despite my not knowing this strange man, I agreed. The conversation flowed easily, he was charming and kind, with a certain old-school chivalry about him. Before long, we arrived outside of my house and only when he took my hand to help me up the steps to the front door of my Victorian townhouse, did I notice that his knuckles were swollen and bloodied, and he had a small cut on his chiselled cheekbone. Now, that just wouldn't do. I am a doctor for goodness sake. Without taking no for an answer, I invited him inside and insisted on fixing his wounds. He laughed and followed my lead up to the bathroom. Climbing the steep, creaking stairs, we took the opportunity to introduce ourselves. To my surprise, he told me his name was Frederick; he looked far too young for such an ancient name. When I pointed that out, he revealed that he came from a very traditional family and he was named after his great-grandfather. It's something I, a woman named Joy after my grandmother, could fully understand. Frederick remarked that Joy was a suitable name for a woman such as myself and that I embodied the name perfectly. Heat rose to my cheeks from the embarrassment of such a compliment. No amount of concussion could convince me that I was not years too old for the poor man, but his compliment was welcome anyhow.

In the bathroom, I prepared the necessary ointments and wipes to clean his wounds and warned him it could sting a little. Like men do, he shrugged it off. Then, the most peculiar occurrence took place. As I gently wiped the blood from his knuckles, it revealed perfectly healed skin beneath. Curiously, I dabbed the cut on his cheek, his eyes never leaving mine, watching me intently. It was an intense moment that seemed to stretch time. Although, my confusion broke the trance as I could not fathom how he had healed already. "It was probably just the man's blood. It would make sense, I'm not in any pain." He said, explaining away the conundrum. I remained sceptical but who was I to call him a liar?

No further medical attention required, he made his excuses to leave and I showed him to the door. All the while pondering the strange encounter. Opening the door, he paused in the entrance and faced me, smiling sweetly. Frederick asked if he could see me again and butterflies erupted in my tummy like I was fifteen again. Face blushing and heart racing, I agreed. Maybe this old soul could feel young enough again to make a new friend, I thought.

It's 7:30pm now; I fear I'm running out of time. This next part will be brief, in order to get it all down.

The next time we met, we found ourselves seated in the most fashionable restaurant in town. Frederick was dressed in a finely pressed, dark grey suit with a navy and burnt orange paisley pocket square. He looked dashing. Ever the gentleman, he complimented my burgundy dress and floral shawl and I just knew my cheeks matched my attire. I wasn't used to such compliments. We each ordered the same dish of steak and confit potatoes with roasted vine tomatoes. Mouth-watering and taste buds tingling, I devoured the dish in no time, humming and cooing over the delicious flavours. All the while listening to Frederick tell wonderfully detailed stories about his journeys around the world. It was thrilling. Yet, I was half distracted by him continuously chopping up his food and not a single forkful entering his mouth. He manoeuvred the food around his plate, theatrically sharing his *experience climbing the pyramids of Egypt, still not a single bite was swallowed. Upon asking Frederick if there was anything wrong with his dish and offering to send it back and order something different, he apologised and admitted he was too nervous to stomach anything. We laughed it off together and I assured him he did not need to feel such a way with me. Regardless though, he did not finish his food and we settled the bill and headed home.*

    The few times we met thereafter, more strange behaviour ensued. For example, we only ever met at night. My busy schedule usually only allows for evenings but occasionally I'd have a whole day free and despite him not having to work, he still only made himself available after dark.
    Three months after initially meeting that fateful night, my friends invited him round for trivia night. He eagerly agreed and we showed up, wine bottle in hand, prepared to win. My lovely friend, June, swung the door open, brightly smiling and squeezing me tightly as I entered the house. Only when I gestured to introduce Frederick, he remained standing in the entranceway with a panicked look upon his face. After several awkward moments, June snorted with laughter and invited the silly bugger in because he was letting all the cold air in. Deep in muddled thoughts and heavily distracted

by the bizarre behaviour I lost drastically and uncharacteristically at game night. It was highly embarrassing and my biggest defeat yet.

    Shortly after, on a warm summer evening, Frederick joined me at 10pm (after dark) for some tapas and s'mores. While dicing onions, the prickly juices stung my eyes and in my hazy vision the knife slipped and sliced my finger. It burned like hell and I yelped before running it under the tap. Frederick leapt from his chair at the dining table, white as a ghost and bolted out the door. There I was, a tiny cut on my finger and he all but passed out. In my confusion, I texted the insane man to joke about him either being squeamish or being a vampire because they are the only two explanations for such a reaction. An hour later when he hadn't replied, I texted him again to express my concern and that I hoped he was ok.

    He never did reply. It was awfully confusing and two weeks later anger had replaced any worry I felt. It dawned on me then that I didn't even know where he lived. He was still as much of a mystery to me now as he was when we met. The only things I knew about him were superficial.

    Without a second thought, I marched out of my house and headed for The Midnight Bar, remembering the importance of the place on the night we met. Storming into the poorly lit tavern, I furiously scanned each wonky table for the tall man, with dark hair and feline eyes. But there was no sign of him. Stomping out with no idea where to go next, you'll forgive my language when I tell you that my eyes couldn't fathom the fucking monstrosity unfolding before me. In the alleyway next to the bar, the most god-awful sight played out under the streetlamp. Frederick was pressing a woman up against the wall, face buried in her neck as she was moaning. Acid churned in my stomach. We were not lovers by any stretch, but we were respectable companions, enjoying each other's company. Sometimes sensually while we shared red wine and stories of our past. And now here I was, dumfounded, with a front-row seat to him devouring this woman. Her moans echoing off the alley walls.

Or was it moaning?

With immense effort, I calmed the sound of my heart beating in my eardrums and listened more closely. She was most certainly not moaning; she was crying out for help! My feet took off before my brain could catch up. Within seconds I was upon them, prising him off her, elbowing my way between them and calling out his name.

Eventually, he snapped out of it, pulled away and the woman slid to the floor. Her eyes rolled into the back of her head, sweat beading on her brows and blood gushing from her neck. The tension in the air was palpable, nobody moved. I knelt next to the poor woman, who was sickly white and watched in horror as she gasped her last breath. Slowly, I glared up at Frederick, adrenaline surging through my veins. His mouth was smeared with blood, dripping from his chin and his eyes were bloodshot. The terror of that image still haunts me all these weeks later. Again my feet were racing away faster than I could think to flee for safety. I didn't stop until I reached my front door, frantically unlocking it and barricading myself inside.

Fumbling for my house phone, I dialled the police and left an anonymous tip explaining that there was a woman in the alley by The Midnight Bar who needed help and I hung up. Then I stumbled to my bedroom, panting and mumbling, trying to make sense of what I had just witnessed.

I'm not sure how much longer I can keep them at bay. Bear with me while I bring us to the present tense.

A few days later, my heart finally started to beat normally again and I devised a plan. This was where things got tricky. I texted Frederick asking him to come over to talk things through. I explained that I knew he wouldn't hurt me and that if he cared about me he would tell me the truth about himself.

An agonisingly slow couple of minutes passed before he responded to accept my invitation. That evening, he arrived late. I assume he felt the need to ensure there were no police here ready to intercept and arrest him. I wouldn't have done that to him. He was my friend, and I had other plans.

His fist gently tapped on the door and I undid each of the three bolts and peered my head around the chain. His look of defeat had my heart racing and my eyes watering. His sunken eyes displayed his lack of sleep and his grim expression tugged on my heartstrings. He was no monster, but he was dangerous. Shutting the door, I unlatched the chain and opened the door wider, gesturing for him to enter. As he stepped inside, the corners of his mouth twitched upwards and his gaze softened with gratitude. Until his eyes rolled into the back of his head and he collapsed clumsily to the floor.

Mouth agape in disbelief that it worked, I trod carefully over the shards of broken glass and wilted roses to close the door. Regret immediately sunk in as I struggled to drag his dead weight to the basement where his head rhythmically bashed into each step on the way down. I cringed with each steady beat.

With a tremendous amount of effort, I hoisted him onto the wooden table and laid him on his back. Frederick didn't flinch once as I spread his arms to the side and straightened his legs. Fear gripped my insides as I panicked about him waking up when I hammered a sharp wooden stake into his hand to pin him to the table. He stirred and groaned, rolling his head to the side, but did not fully regain consciousness.

After each stake was secured into his arms and ankles I prepared a mild tranquilliser to keep at hand for when he awoke. A perk of working in a hospital, free drugs if you're willing to break the law.

Hours passed by and tiredness crept in but I had to remain on high alert. Eventually, his eyes fluttered open and anxiety took hold as he realised the position he was in. In the most soothing voice I could muster, I calmly urged him to relax and injected the tranquilliser. It wasn't enough to knock him out, but it was the right amount to calm his nerves and keep him still. Pulling out my notebook, I began my line of questioning. Are you a vampire? Do they exist? How do they exist? You know, all the usual questions one might have after seeing a man suck the life out of a woman via two holes in her neck.

My notebook is hidden in the third floorboard from the wall in my bedroom by the door. Retrieve it and take it to anyone who will listen.

Once I had exhausted all my questions and Frederick looked too tired to answer anymore, I had made up my mind that I needed more scientific research. To Frederick's credit, he answered everything in detail and I am still inclined to believe every word. But I needed more concrete evidence. The only way I could conceivably get the answers I needed was to take a look at his brain.

That brings me to now. It's been three weeks since I started operating on Frederick and I believe I have all the answers I've been looking for. The poor guy is exhausted beyond belief but he's been a good sport, very accommodating, despite his threats to kill me once he is free. Now I do not know what to do with him. He can enter my house! There is no barricade strong enough to keep him out. But I am no murderer, I'm just a surgeon, a surgeon who knows everything there is to know about vampires. I cannot die before my findings reach the outside world.

One more minor problem I must mention- I am being attacked by other vampires. I am unsure how they found out that Fredrick was here or that he was incapacitated but they know and they have been terrorising me for three weeks!

Each night when I go to bed, these demonic creatures, who cannot enter my house uninvited, taunt and threaten me. I am trapped in my home. Haunted by my discovery. I cannot call the police, they will think I'm mad. I have not left my bedroom in two days for fear that Frederick will attack me.

The knocking on my window has started already so I must go now.
If you are reading this, please publish my findings. Let the world know what I discovered and destroy them all to ensure our safety.
If I am here but not myself, please put me out of my misery. I do not wish to be this way and do not wish to harm anyone.
And if after all of this, I am no longer alive, please bury me next to my mother in the graveyard by the church.

Sincerely,
Joy

It's 8:30pm and I sign my letter with a flourish and tuck it into an envelope. I stand up from my desk and head over to my window where there are smears of blood oozing down the windowpane. A bat-like creature swooshes past, startling me. As I leap backwards something catches my eye on the pavement. June. She is heading up the steps to my front door. I must let her in, I'll be damned if they bring her any harm.
With careful movements, I unlock the many

locks on my bedroom door. Creep down the stairs, holding my breath and approach the front door. I take a moment to listen carefully; Frederick is silent and likely too weak to cry out for help. Anxiety bubbles in my gut as I methodically unlock the front door and open it quickly urging June to come in.

She jumps in and I desperately secure the door.

"What's going on? Why the urgency?" June asks, concerned.

"You will never believe me. Come on, you must come upstairs with me. I have so much to tell you." My voice is hoarse and my hands tremble as if the temperature has just dropped suddenly in the hallway.

We race up the stairs and I all but shove June into my bedroom and secure the door. When I turn around it all comes tumbling out. Everything that has happened in the last six months. The words escape so fast, I can barely catch a breath and I pray June is following enough to understand my fear.

When I have finished explaining the insane events that have unfolded, she studies me for a moment. I reach out and grab her hand, pleading with her to believe a word I have said. It takes a second to register, but when it does I recoil. June's hand is ice cold. I meet her gaze and her blank stare makes my blood run cold.

"June. Are you well? You're freezing?" I ask, a sense of danger creeping into my bones. June takes a step forward and the hairs on the back of my neck spike. A light knocking on the window distracts me and when I look, Frederick is floating midair, glaring right at me with a disturbing smile on his pale face. *What have I done?*

Returning to June, she nods toward Frederick and then steps closer to me again. Instinctively, I step back only to meet with the door, the cold metal of the locks a shock to my system, all my nerves on high alert. June steps closer again, leaning in to whisper in my ear. I brace myself for what she is about to say but nothing comes. And it dawns on me that it's not my ear she was reaching for.

New Friends, New Sins

Sitting on a cushion in the middle of the beige room, Megan looks around at the bland space, wondering how she ended up here. This suffocating and uncomfortable room couldn't be more different to Megan's pink, floral decor, and cluttered shelves and boxes with years' worth of books, makeup and clothes overflowing onto the floor. There is no personality in this space; it's almost clinical. The bed is perfectly made with white bedding and various shaped decorative pillows; the walls are colour-drenched in light beige with panelling that gives it the impression of being a guest room, not the room of a sixteen-year-old. The tall, white wardrobe in the corner blends into the other boring decor and the only bit of colour is a pink mouse and keyboard on Chloe's wooden desk. Megan wonders whose idea it was to decorate the room like this and finds it hard to believe that Chloe didn't have to petition to get a colourful mouse and keyboard.

In the three days since she was invited to this sleepover, Megan hasn't managed to work out why. Chloe has made it her life's mission to make Megan's last three years at school a living hell; Rachel has been nothing but mean to her and has egged Chloe on every step of the way; and Emily hasn't so much as smiled at Megan since they started at Mulberry Academy. Until now, when all three of them sat down in the middle of Chloe's bedroom for a Halloween slumber party.

Megan didn't want to come; she protested to her mum every waking minute after telling her about the invite and begged the whole car journey for her mother to turn around and take her home. But her mum insisted this was a good opportunity to make some friends, and that if she could just try, she might enjoy herself. Though, when they arrived at the house, she did tack on that she was only a phone call away if it was that bad. So, Megan reluctantly dragged herself out of the car and now here she was, waiting for the fun to start.

"I think we should play a game," Rachel suggests.

"Like what?" Emily asks.

"I know! Let's play truth or dare," Chloe says. The other's agree enthusiastically and Megan nods nervously. She hopes to God that they don't ask her anything embarrassing and she prays even harder that they don't make her do anything she doesn't want to do. It's hard to say no to girls like these because they don't understand the word.

Rachel goes first and she's almost giddy at the anticipation of what might happen. She opts to tell a truth and Chloe instructs Megan to ask her something. She racks her brain, trying to think of something exciting or interesting to ask and panics when nothing springs to mind. She hates being put on the spot. Her mind goes blank and Chloe urges her to hurry up.

"What's the naughtiest thing you have ever done?" She blurts it out and then cringes at her rubbish question. The others ponder for a moment and then Chloe announces that she knows the answer and giggles before whispering in Rachel's ear.

"Oh yes, that's it!" Rachel grins. "We were actually playing this game last summer in the park and as we were leaving Thomas gave me a dare. He dared me to kick a homeless man sleeping in the underpass, so obviously I did it! It was so funny, he started screaming at us and we all had to leg it!" She laughs, and Chloe and Emily join in. Megan is stunned at their awful sense of humour and can't believe they would treat someone like that.

"You're savage!" Chloe tells her. Rachel looks proud after receiving the praise and Megan asks her why she would do that.

"It was only a joke. I didn't kick him *that*

hard. Anyway, my parents say that homeless people are society's waste and they deserve whatever they get," she says.

"Do you really believe that? Homeless people are still humans. They just need extra help and care." Megan defends quietly.

"Of course not," Rachel agrees unconvincingly and shares a not-so-discreet side eye with Chloe.

"Ok, let's do a fun one now. Megan, it's your turn." Chloe announces, obliterating the awkward tension. Megan picks truth because it feels like the safer option and she figures she can tell a white lie if necessary. Chloe asks her if she has ever kissed a boy in a tone that suggests she knows she hasn't. Megan chooses to be honest as she is not ashamed to have never kissed a boy. Impressing boys doesn't feel like a priority right now and since school will be over soon, it's unlikely that she will stay in contact with anyone when she goes to college in the neighbouring town.

She instantly regrets her decision as they all burst into fits of judgemental giggles and a sliver of shame creeps in. Chloe divulges her first kiss story with one of the cute boys from her horse riding club. She swoons over how dreamy he is but says his parents are too strict to let him have a girlfriend at this age. So, they secretly make out when they get the chance in the stables and no one is looking. Chloe says it's good practice for when she meets a real man. Emily then tells the group about her first kiss. It was with a friend she's had since primary school and they had play dates as children. She smiles sweetly as she reminisces about how nervous they both were. But they wanted to get their first kiss out of the way and decided who better to do it with than each other since they had known each other forever. The kiss was awkward and sloppy but it ignited a spark and they've been secretly dating ever since. Envy replaces the shame that Megan was feeling and she starts to doubt whether her choice to avoid boys was a good one after all. She feels inexperienced and a little left behind. It hadn't occurred to her that everyone would be so ready for all this stuff, but now she is wondering if going to college having never kissed a boy will make her a loser. She bites her lower lip, contemplating. But then she remembers what her mother always said to her about how she was so glad she waited for the right person to come along because when she met her first boyfriend in college, she got to explore all those embarrassing firsts with someone she could trust and take it slow with. Megan lightens up a bit at the memory and tells the girls she wants to wait for the right boy. Chloe and Rachel snigger at her but Emily tells her she's glad she did the same.

"I'm bored now. This game is not as fun as it was last time. Emily, you go next but you have to do a dare," Rachel groans. Emily reluctantly agrees. "Good. What shall we make her do?" Rachel asks.

"I know," Chloe chimes in. "Remember last time you came, Emily? You had some of my mum's cake and said how much you loved it?" Emily nods apprehensively. "Well, she made one for tonight. You should eat it all!" Chloe's grin almost touches her ears but doesn't reach her eyes. Megan shudders and fidgets uncomfortably on her cushion. "Eat a whole cake? That's a weird dare, but I bet you can't do it," Rachel says.

"Um… ok. I can try," Emily chuckles lightly. Chloe claps and runs downstairs to retrieve the cake. Her mum is on the phone in the kitchen and shoos her out of the way before storming out and going to the living room. Chloe ignores her and stomps back up the stairs with a huge chocolate cake and a fork in hand. She places it on the floor in front of Emily and warns her not to drop any on the polished laminate floor. Megan and Emily's eyes go wide at the size of the cake. It is enough to feed at least eight people. Emily loves cake and assumes she will be able to eat a bit and then they'll get bored and want to move on, so she picks up the fork and digs in.

A short while later, she slows her forkfuls and the cake coats her mouth in a dry sugary paste. Her cheeks flush pink as the pressure to keep going starts to build.

"Don't stop. You need to finish it. I dared you and if you don't you'll have to do a forfeit," Chloe warns. Emily looks up but doesn't say a word. A forfeit would be something horrible. She knew it because she had been forced to do one before, where they made her run into a shop and pull her shirt up exposing herself to everyone inside. She felt humiliated and degraded but fortunate that her tiny boobs were covered by a sports bra and the other two didn't notice. They gave her so much praise for being a daredevil after that they forgot all about the original dare and she was grateful they weren't disappointed in her. The silent treatment was their worst punishment. It made her feel invisible.

"You don't have to finish it if you don't want to," Megan offers, but Emily just laughs uncomfortably and carries on until it's all gone and she looks visibly ill. Chloe congratulates her and remarks that she could never do that because her tiny tummy couldn't possibly fit it in. Rachel agrees and they enter into a competition about who eats less. Megan watches in confusion at the two of them bragging about their unhealthy eating habits. Suddenly, Emily jumps up and races out of the room. The other two go into fits of laughter about how she couldn't handle a bit of cake and what a good dare it was.

When Emily comes back she looks haggard and sweaty and Megan asks her if she's okay. "I'm fine. At least I'll be skinnier now," she jokes. "I doubt it," Rachel mumbles under her breath.

Chloe goes last and she chooses to do a dare. Megan dares her to go and make her mum jump downstairs. Since it is Halloween, she said it would be funny and on theme, but secretly thought it would also be harmless.

They all wait at the top of the staircase while Chloe creeps down each step, careful not to make a sound. She pauses at the bottom and listens for where her mother is, assuming she is still in the living room. Tiptoeing down the hallway she stops just outside the door. Her mother is still rambling on the phone but Chloe can't work out who she could be talking to.

Rachel, who has descended halfway down the stairs, urges her to get it over with, so Chloe nudges the door slightly, slides in through the small gap and crouches next to the sofa. Her mum doesn't notice and Chloe prepares to leap up and surprise her. Only, something her mum says stops her in her tracks. She overhears her mum gushing over the person on the other end, laughing at whatever they have said, and then her blood turns to ice as she hears her mum call the person Steve. She has no clue who this Steve is but she is sure her mother just told him she loves him before hanging up the phone.

 For a second Chloe is confused about why her mother would be telling a man, who is not her father, that she loves him. Then it dawns on her that she's heard that name before. A few months ago, a new employee at work took the ladies in the office by surprise with his good looks and charm, *and he was single*. She remembers her mum talking about how the other women in the office were throwing themselves at him even though he was far too young for them all. Blood rushes to her ears; her mother must be one of those women. Sensing the impatience of the girls, she half-heartedly leaps up and shouts boo. Her mother gasps and yells at her to go to her room, stating that she only let her have friends over so she'd be left alone.

The girls are disappointed by the lack of her mother's reaction but Emily quickly realises something is off with Chloe and asks her what's wrong. Back in the bedroom, Chloe's brother, Sam, comes in wanting to know what all the fuss was downstairs. A tearful Chloe snaps at him to leave them alone and go and play his games since all he cares about is his computer. He demands an answer and they all urge her to spill whatever happened. Chloe tells them all what she heard and Megan calmly expresses that it could be nothing. She could have been joking to him after he helped her with some work or it could have been someone else. She knows her suggestions are likely not helping or true, but watching Chloe tear up as she recounted her mum's conversation made Megan feel sorry for her. No one should have to witness their mum cheating on their dad.

Sam looks at her with a guilty expression like there's something he knows. Everyone waits with bated breath for him to spill the beans. He tells them about how he came home from school early a couple of weeks ago because he wasn't feeling well, and when he came in, Steve was in the kitchen with their mother. When they heard the front door, they clambered around and Steve left in a hurry.

Sam explains that his mum told him Steve was coming to quote for some plumbing that needed doing in the kitchen but Sam wasn't convinced because Steve was dressed in a fancy suit. He didn't say anything because he didn't want to tell Dad and things to blow up because of him.

Chloe tells him that he did the right thing and that she will tell their dad the next day when he gets home from his work trip. She lays her hand on Sam's arm, gives it a reassuring squeeze and then tells him to go back to his game to have one last normal night before things turn upside down.

The three friends watch uncomfortably and Megan wishes she could go home and tell her mum everything. She debates whether to tell them she doesn't feel well and see if she can get her mum to come and collect her but a small part of her wants to stay and comfort Chloe if she needs it.

"Chloe, you shouldn't say anything to your dad. I saw my dad kissing a woman outside of a restaurant in town when I came out of the cinema one night and he paid me a thousand pounds not to tell my mum. I bought a brand new Yves Saint Laurent bag and forgot all about it. They're adults, they're going to do stupid things and then bribe us not to say anything. It's better than breaking up your family," Rachel says like it would be Chloe's fault her parents break up if her dad finds out about her mum's affair.

"Whatever. Let's just talk about something else," Chloe replies.

"Oh, I know. It's Halloween, so obviously we have to do at least one scary thing. And since you're all too chicken to watch a scary film, I brought this.," Rachel says, pulling a large piece of cardboard from her bag.

The girls shriek when Rachel lays a Ouija board on the floor with a mischievous smile. Emily says there is no way she is messing with that and Chloe tells her not to be so silly and superstitious and gets up to light some candles in the room for the extra ambience. Rachel also turns out the light, so they are shrouded in darkness and flickering candlelight. Megan gets goosebumps before anything has even happened and feels stupid for being freaked out by it. She has never believed in ghosts or spirits so she knows this is a stupid game but it doesn't stop her heart from thumping loudly in her chest.

Rachel pulls a small card out of her bag and silences the room. In her most official voice, she reads the statement. "I invite the spirits to come to us and share their message. I am now opening the lines of communication and welcome them to enter this home. Let your presence be known." A chill runs up Megan's spine and she shudders at the eerie feeling that has descended on the room. Nervous giggles erupt between the group and Chloe grabs the plastic cursor and encourages everyone to hold it with her on the board. Each girl hesitantly places their finger down and Rachel asks into the room if there is anyone with them now. The plastic slowly moves towards the word yes written on the top left corner of the board and they all gasp and squeal. Rachel then admits it was her and instructs them all to start again.

"Is the devil in the room with us?" Chloe asks in a haunting voice. They all pause and wait for the black token to move and this time it inches towards the word no on the right. They all sigh with relief, looking around the room and at each other waiting for someone to admit that it was them who moved the piece. All of a sudden, a candle near the window flickers out and the four of them scream and huddle together. Emily clutches her chest and leaps up to turn on the light.

"I don't like this. Let's do something else," she pleads.

"Don't be silly, it probably just ran out of wax or some breeze from outside blew it out. Ghosts aren't real, you idiot," Rachel dismisses. A tiny hiccup escapes Megan and they all laugh at her. "I must have screamed a bit too hard," she giggles. "That was quite freaky."

"Stop being wusses. Let's do it again," Chloe demands. They carry on, asking silly questions into the void and take it in turns to move the token around the board, scaring each other. Nothing else happens and eventually, they get bored of the lack of action and decide to watch a funny film to shake off any remaining fear still lingering from trying to connect with evil spirits.

Tucked into their blow-up beds, they chat about real-life scary things they've witnessed and whether they believe ghosts are real. The room is divided and Megan can't wrap her head around whether Chloe and Rachel are joking about believing in spirits. Eventually, they drift off to sleep one by one and the film plays in the background, lighting up the room so no scary beings can lurk in the dark.

A few hours later a buzzing sound coming from the static on the TV wakes Emily and she sits up in bed looking for the remote on the floor. She is startled when the floppy form of

Megan standing on the opposite side of the room catches her attention. Heart racing, she looks around to see if the other two are awake and wonders if they are messing with her.

"Megan? Are you okay?" Emily whispers. Megan doesn't move, she just stands awkwardly leaning with her head to the side and eyes wide open. Emily watches her, waiting for the joke to land but no one moves to make her jump and Megan remains like a statue, without so much as blinking.

"Megan, you're scaring me now. Stop it," Emily begs. From the light on the TV, she can see that Megan's eyes aren't moving and the hairs on the back of her neck stand on end. She leans over, not wanting to take her eye off Megan and shakes Chloe attempting to wake her up. Chloe doesn't stir and Emily shoves her harder, and when she doesn't open her eyes, bile rises to Emily's throat. Slowly looking back at Megan, she hasn't moved.

The room grows cold and Megan's eyes appear more glazed over than before. The demonic figure looms in the corner and panic starts to take hold of Emily and she frantically tries to wake Rachel on the other side of her. She recoils when her hand meets Rachel's cool skin and tears brim in her eyes. Emily braces herself to look away from Megan and at the two lifeless girls on either side of her. When she looks harder at Chloe in the dim light, a dark outline forms on the pillow underneath her head. She tentatively reaches over to touch it and shrieks when her hand comes back coated in damp red liquid. Scrambling to her feet, she leans towards Rachel and gasps when she notices her mouth stuffed with the corner of her blanket. Immediately, Emily releases the remaining contents of her stomach onto the inflatable mattress and awkwardly gets off the semi-deflated bed as the vomit begins to slide towards her feet.

  Daring to look back at Rachel she sees that there are coins and notes placed around her head but is too terror-stricken to work out what that means. Slowly peering towards Megan again, the horrifying scene before her finally settles in and Emily wails and bolts towards the door. She prays that this is just a horrible dream, but the cool laminate floor on her feet and blood-stained hand confirms this is very real.

  Barging out of the bedroom, the crack in Sam's door reveals another terrible sight. His limp body is slumped in his gaming chair and for a second she hopes he is asleep. Until she sees the crimson puddle on the floor and her heart sinks to her feet. There is no time to dwell on the image as Chloe's bedroom door handle creaks downwards and the door steadily opens. Emily backs up towards the stairs, eyes wide when Megan's form fills the doorway. Her head is bent at an odd angle and her legs shuffle awkwardly like she has no control over her body. Emily rattles off a prayer hoping to release the devil possessing the girl in front of her but it doesn't work. Megan gains on her, reaching her arm out to grab Emily. She rushes down the stairs two steps at a time, shouting for Chloe's mother. At the bottom of the stairs, she braves a look behind her and Megan's zombie-like body is struggling to make it down.

    Returning her focus to getting out of this godforsaken house, she races past the living room, stopping when she sees the lifeless body of Mrs Rotherford sprawled on the floor. A huge knife protrudes from her chest and her eyes are glaring at the ceiling. Emily sobs, cupping her hand over her mouth at the bloody sight. When she blinks away her tears she notices the writing on the mirror above the fireplace. *Whore* is smeared in blood on the otherwise pristine mirror. Emily's knees wobble and threaten to give out when a crash descends the stairs. Nervously peaking round the doorframe, Emily staggers back when

Megan's body cracks and snaps into place as she stands back up from a broken huddle on the floor. Emily can't believe what she is seeing, won't believe it. There is no way this is real. The devil isn't real and her friend isn't possessed. They are all playing a huge, elaborate trick on her. They have to be. The alternative is too far-fetched, too terrifying.

She can't take that risk though, so she runs to the front door, frantically trying to unlock it but there is no key and it's not hung up on a hook on the wall like in her house, and looking around, there is no bowl on a table or draw for them to be tucked inside of. She pounds relentlessly on the door, shouting for someone to help and pulling the door handle trying to prise it open. A sense of her space becoming smaller creeps in from behind and Emily looks over her shoulder. Megan's slack face is staring right into her soul and she backs up against the door, still banging her fists against it.

Megan has a fork tightly gripped in her hand and Emily lets out a deafening scream, hoping to alert someone, anyone, to what is happening. She squeezes herself into the corner, trying to make herself as small as possible, her legs growing weaker as fear consumes her.

"No. No! Help me," she cries, shaking and

panting. Every last shred of hope drains from her heart and she buries her head into her knees, whispering a prayer repeatedly. Megan looms above, fork in hand and plunges into Emily over and over. Each withdrawal sends blood splattering up the door and walls and Emily assumes a defensive position as each blow pierces her skin. She tries to scramble out of the corner and away from the demonic creature, but as she crawls on her hands and knees, Megan pushes her to the floor and straddles her. Arms pinned to the ground under Megan's knees, and with no strength left to fight her off, Emily continues muttering prayers, eyes wide, as Megan forces the fork into her neck and yanks it out. Gurgling blood bubbles and seeps out of the puncture wounds and Emily's mouth fills with blood. She coughs and sputters as her airways fill with ruby liquid that splashes over her cheeks and down to the floor. Megan remains on top of her until the spits of blood slow down and retreat into Emily's throat.

    Megan ungracefully stands up and limps to the kitchen where she turns on the gas stove, letting the air fill with the invisible poison. Then she patiently sits at the dining table and waits, never blinking or twitching a muscle. As the gas starts to reduce the oxygen around her,

Megan collapses face-first to the table.

A while later, an intermittent beeping sounds in Megan's ears. Her head pounds as she gently sits up and looks about the room. She wonders how she made it into the kitchen and panics as she realises that she must have sleep walked again. She cringes with embarrassment, hoping she didn't disturb anyone. This only ever happens when she sleeps in unfamiliar places.

Pulling out from the dining table, a red handprint remains where she pushed the table. She slowly holds her hands up to her face and the blood drains from her cheeks as she realises what is coating her hands. Looking down at the rest of her outfit, the rips and stains have her reeling. She can't remember anything after they finished playing with the Ouija board. Megan briefly wonders if the girls have played a Halloween trick on her and are trying to scare her using fake blood, but the house is so eerily quiet and she knows in her heart that something is seriously wrong.

Creeping into the hallway, the first thing she spots is two feet lying still on the floor by the front door. Unsure who it is, she edges closer until Emily's distorted face comes into view. "Emily?" she asks, trembling. When

Emily doesn't respond, Megan starts hyperventilating and can't catch her breath. She rushes down the hall to where she saw the house phone when she arrived earlier in the evening and it's not there. She remembers that Chloe has an old mobile phone in her room, so she runs upstairs to find it.

When she reaches the bedroom, the TV is still blaring brightly with static and the two silhouettes of Chloe and Rachel lie still in their beds. Megan falls to the floor, unable to comprehend what has happened in this horrific house. A huge wave of dread crashes into her, knocking the wind out of her lungs. She knows she has to go deeper into the room to get the phone, but every part of her body is yelling to get out. Looking around the room, a rush of nausea hits her and she momentarily has to sit down to steady herself. She inhales a few large breaths to help ease the dizziness, but it doesn't help.

From her spot on the bed, she glimpses the silver flip phone by Chloe's head and stumbles over to it. When she gets hold of it, she flips it open and fights her brain to recall her mother's number. Megan weakly punches in the numbers, the drowsiness making her sway like a ship on a rough sea. With every number she pushes, her strength declines, until the phone falls out of her hand.

    Crashing to her knees to retrieve it, another wave of light-headedness comes barreling down and Megan hits the floor. The half-typed number is displayed on the screen as she stares ahead glassy-eyed and unable to move. A distorted figure forms in front of her and the sound of hooves clopping on the laminate echoes around her. Its sinister goat-like face grins at her while she slips deeper into unconsciousness. Shallow, wheezy breaths are all she can muster as the amount of oxygen in the room continues to diminish. Euphoria envelops her and she closes her eyes to embrace it.

Thank You

I want to say a massive thank you for reading my short stories. I hope they were as heart-wrenching and spine-tingling for you as they were for my mum.

If you would like to support me, please follow me on social media and look out for future releases.

Instagram + Threads + TikTok = **@vobymaraya**

www.ingramcontent.com/pod-product-compliance
Ingram Content Group UK Ltd.
Pitfield, Milton Keynes, MK11 3LW, UK
UKHW030634130325
456214UK00006B/184